The Matchmaker's Mare

by

Hywela Lyn

Copyright Notice
This is a work of fiction. Names, characters, places, and incidents are either the product of the author's imagination or are used fictitiously, and any resemblance to actual persons living or dead, business establishments, events, or locales, is entirely coincidental.

The Matchmaker's Mare

COPYRIGHT © 2024 by Hywela Lyn

All rights reserved. No part of this book may be used or reproduced in any manner whatsoever including the purpose of training artificial intelligence technologies in accordance with Article 4(3) of the Digital Single Market Directive 2019/790, The Wild Rose Press expressly reserves this work from the text and data mining exception. Only brief quotations embodied in critical articles or reviews may be allowed.
Contact Information: info@thewildrosepress.com

Cover Art by *Teddi Black*

The Wild Rose Press, Inc.
PO Box 708
Adams Basin, NY 14410-0708
Visit us at www.thewildrosepress.com

Publishing History
First Edition, 2025
Trade Paperback ISBN 978-1-5092-5988-5
Digital ISBN 978-1-5092-5989-2

Published in the United States of America

Dedication

For my late husband David Evans, who did the 'heavy horse-work' for me, enabling me to make time to write this book, and John Evans, my first husband, who died tragically young and would have been so thrilled that I wrote this story, also for my lovely friends, Sara, Neil and Oliver Robertson, and Julie and Bill Gabis. I honestly don't know what I would do without all your help and support.

And for all the horses I've owned, especially Star, Flicka, and Tiptop (aka 'Flying T'pau') who gave their names to some of the horses in this story, not forgetting Smokey, Mr Fifty, Sally, and Harri).

Finally, remembering my dear sister, Christine Summers, who shared my love of all creatures 'great and small', and is sorely missed.

Acknowledgements

No novel sees the light of day through the efforts of one person alone, and huge thanks go to my editor, Frances Sevilla. Heartfelt thanks also to Kathy Noyes, who read and gave invaluable feedback and suggestions, to Debby, Elinor, Eleanor and Bill, of the crit group 'Bobby's Gang', who gave such useful feedback and support, and to Lynn Griffin and Rachael Richey, fellow British 'Wild Roses' who both also read and critiqued my final drafts and offered much appreciated insight and suggestions.

Prologue

Near Pentrebont, West Wales, sometime in the distant past.

"Faster Seren, faster." Leaning low over the pony's neck the young woman urged her into a mile-eating gallop. The mare's hooves scarcely seemed to touch the ground as she appeared to fly across the rugged landscape. If only Seren really could gallop through the air, it would make her escape so much easier.

There had been something very special about the filly Rhiannon found as a motherless foal in the mountains and raised until fully grown. She named her *Seren*, meaning 'Star', for the perfect diamond-shaped star on her face. Seren needed no breaking-in or training, but allowed Rhiannon to sit on her back as soon as she was mature enough to take a rider. No one else could ride her, not even Sion Sienco. Now she could only hope the mare would carry her to Sion in time.

She cast one last, swift look over her shoulder at the only home she had ever known. The cottage receded into the distance, appearing forlorn in the soft moonlight before melting into the darkness. She could almost believe the cottage knew she would never return. With a sigh, she turned her head to concentrate on the rough road ahead.

Thoughts of the injured animals the villagers, or their children, would bring to the cottage for her to heal flashed into her mind, and hot tears stung her eyes. Her spells and herbs could heal most injuries provided they were not too severe. Now she would no longer be able to help them. Nor would she be able to use her gift of matchmaking to help the maidens in the village find their one true love. "Oh Sion," she whispered, "Sion, where are you when I need you?"

She pushed the mare even faster. "Sion," she whispered once more. "Sion, please let me find you."

Her father's harsh words rang in her head and a shiver ran through her, which had nothing to do with the chill night air. "It is all arranged. You will marry Gwynfor Pryce. We have already agreed on the marriage settlement and the wedding will take place a week today. There will be no more argument."

Rhiannon knew then she must leave the little cottage where she had lived with her father since her mother died five years before. Leaving the dwelling where she'd lived her whole life, the only home she knew, made her heart ache. However, she would not marry a man she hated. A man many years her senior, whom she knew to be cruel to his servants and animals.

Along the edge of the forest and past the foot of the craggy *Bryn Glas* mountains they sped. Rhiannon clutched her hand to her breast to feel the reassuring bulk of the kerchief holding the only wealth she possessed—some silver coins, and a small gold ring inherited from her mother. She swung the pony southeast, to follow the drovers' route she knew Sion would take on his return journey. "Faster, Seren," she whispered once more. Her heart thudded in time to the pony's heavy breathing. The tiny silver bells which decorated her girdle jingled as she urged the pony on as fast as she dared over the rough terrain.

At last, Rhiannon drew rein and allowed the pony a few minutes to catch her breath, before setting off again at a canter. She would rather spend the rest of her life with a penniless gypsy like Sion, than be married to a rich old man for whom she cared nothing. A rich old man who, the rumourmongers whispered, was also a mage. Pryce might own extensive lands and possess great wealth, but she shuddered at the mere thought of him touching her. No doubt her father would have squeezed the highest bride price possible from him. He'd sold her like a broodmare or a milk cow.

Well, they were both in for a disappointment. She would not submit to being forced to marry a man she despised. What had her father been thinking? Customary though it might be for a father to arrange his daughter's marriage, giving her no choice in the matter, surely her father could not be blind to Gwynfor Pryce's true nature? A vision of Pryce's cruel features swam into her mind, and she shivered again.

Taking one hand off the reins, she pulled her cloak more tightly around her shoulders and urged Seren into a gallop once more. She must find Sion before daybreak, before her father discovered her absence. Once he did, she knew he would likely follow her to bring her back. The further away she and Sion could get, the more chance they had of eluding him and starting a new life together. She drew in a deep breath. *Please,* she prayed silently. *Please let me find him soon.*

****

The last time Rhiannon and Sion met, he told her

he had Romany family business to attend to on the English border, but he would see her again in three weeks. He'd given her a sprig of fragrant lavender to wear in her hair. Lavender, a symbol of devotion. Even now its scent surrounded her, reminding her of his love.

Having consulted her scrying bowl in secret, before she left the cottage, she knew he would be on his way back now, but still some distance away. Sion Sienco, both the love of her life and her greatest aggravation. When she'd met the young gypsy lad for the first time, at first he teased her and then wooed her. When she feigned disinterest, he took to playing tricks on her, causing her milk cow to go dry, or her hens to take to the water as if they were ducks. As it dawned on her he too had a little white magic, she scolded him until she became hoarse and ran out of words. For some reason, Sion seemed to find this amusing. Then he took her in his arms and kissed her until she was breathless and told her how sorry he was for causing her so much trouble. Of course, she forgave him, as she always would. After all, who could resist the charm of a Welsh gypsy, especially one as handsome and debonair as Sion Sienco? Sometimes she believed he played those silly tricks on her just for the satisfaction they both had when making up.

With only a few hours left before daylight, Rhiannon at last found the clearing where Sion had made his camp. A glowing fire still burned outside the caravan. The chomping of a horse sounded nearby, and she made out the shadowy form of Sion's black cob grazing beneath the trees. Then she spotted Sion, lying on a blanket near the fire. He never did like sleeping indoors, not even in his wagon. He preferred to sleep under the stars whenever the weather permitted, even now, in winter. She leapt from the pony and knelt beside the young man, shaking his shoulder.

"Sion, Sion wake up for goodness sake. I need you to wake up."

Sion raised himself on one elbow, blinking, before sitting upright.

"Rhiannon, *cariad*—beloved one—what are you doing here? Should you not be tucked up in your own bed fast asleep? What is wrong?"

"Sion, listen to me. My father has arranged for me to marry Gwynfor Pryce in a week's time. What am I to do, Sion? I cannot marry him. I will not." She lowered her voice to a whisper.

"You know 'tis you I want, and only you. We have to flee."

Sion threw off his blanket and jumped to his feet. "Rhiannon, my love, I will never let another man have you, not if you love me. Yes, we must get away, ride as swiftly as our horses can carry us. We will find a preacher to marry us, somewhere we are not known. Then we will find a place to settle down far away, where no one will ever find us."

"That sounds like a good plan, Sion, but I fear my father, or even worse, Pryce himself will come after us."

"How will he know which road we have taken?"

"Have you forgotten? Gwynfor Pryce is a mage, or so they say. If I could find you, using a scrying bowl, then surely, he can do the same."

"Then we must get moving fast. Once we have found someone to marry us, he will have no hold over you. Even Gwynfor Pryce will not dare to steal a wife from her husband."

"I hope you are correct, Sion."

The gypsy reached into the caravan and pulled out his horse's saddle and bridle. Whistling to the animal to come to him, he quickly saddled him and sprang into the saddle. "Come, *cariad,* we must ride swiftly," he said, but Rhiannon was already on Seren's back and galloping ahead.

****

Early the next morning, a few hours after sunrise, they passed by a little chapel nestling in the valley. They knocked on the door of the chapel house and begged the clergyman to marry them. Rhiannon produced several of the silver coins and her mother's wedding ring from her kerchief. After a short ceremony, with the minister's wife and daughter as witnesses, Sion slipped the ring on Rhiannon's finger and the minister pronounced them *man and wife.* They thanked him kindly and remounted, keen to put as much distance as possible between them and Rhiannon's father or Pryce. No doubt one or the other, perhaps both, would be following them by now.

They rode toward the next range of mountains, pausing only to rest the horses and let them snatch some mouthfuls of grass, and drink when they found a river or stream. The wind whipped around them coming from the north, bringing with it flurries of snow. They huddled together on the ground when it grew too dark to ride safely, remounting as soon as the sky lightened with the first glow of dawn. Whenever they came across one of the isolated homesteads along the way, they stopped briefly to purchase a loaf of bread or some fruit, which they ate while riding.

The Matchmaker's Mare

On the third day since she fled her home, the snow started to fall in earnest, soon covering the rocky ground in thick drifts. Riding fast became dangerous, forcing them to slow to a walk, and the biting wind stung their faces, making it difficult to see through the swirling snow. After several hours, Seren whickered softly, as if in warning.

Rhiannon turned and looked back, peering through the driving snow. A rider appeared, like a wraith in the distance. "Sion, there is someone following us, it must be either my father or Gwynfor Pryce."

"Make for the woods," Sion yelled, turning his cob in the direction of a thick forest that covered the lower slopes of the steep mountain range known as *Mynyddoedd y Ddraig*—The Dragon Mountains. "Perhaps we may lose him in the trees."

They leaned low over their horses' necks, urging them on as fast as they dared. Both animals were swift and sure-footed, but the deep snow made it impossible for them to increase the distance between them and their pursuer.

They had to slow their mounts again in order to wend their way through the trees, scarcely able to see through the blinding snow which fell all around them. Before they realised it, their follower, revealing himself as Gwynfor Pryce, closed the distance between them and cast a spell over the forest. The trees the lovers thought would hide them, turned traitor, stretching out their branches to twine around the horses' legs. They threw themselves from their saddles, and Sion hacked at the branches with his dagger, while Rhiannon tore at them with ice-cold fingers. At last, they were free. They remounted, and turning away from the treacherous forest, ploughed through the snow, along the narrow track up the precipitous mountainside.

However, the delay had cost them precious minutes, and soon their pursuer caught up with them and they had no means of escape.

Chapter One

A New Start and a Mystery
Megan, Ty Gwyn, near Pentrebont, West Wales. Spring, 2023

Megan Johnson stepped out of her ten-year-old SUV and contemplated the centuries-old stone cottage with its whitewashed walls and slate roof. *Ty Gwyn* nestled in a grove of trees, the branches reaching over its roof on each side as if to keep the little house safe.

Ty Gwyn—White House—was hers. She still found it a little hard to take in. She hesitated for a moment, swallowing a pang of guilt. Perhaps she shouldn't be so happy to have inherited the cottage. After all, she'd been very fond of dear Great Uncle Thomas. Although he had been in his late eighties, his death still came as something of a shock, as did the solicitor's letter informing her of her inheritance. She'd never really considered the possibility he might leave his cottage to her but apparently, she was now his only living relative.

After removing her suitcase, she locked the vehicle and walked up the winding path to the front porch, graced by an old but solid wooden bench. Early clumps of yellow daffodils, like splashes of sunshine, lined the path, valiantly trying to avoid being stifled by the weeds.

Memories flooded in of frequent childhood visits to Wales; memories of herself sitting on the bench, while her mother helped Uncle Thomas prepare supper.

She allowed herself a soft smile. This place emanated such a peaceful atmosphere, a far cry from the noise and bustle of London. The family moved there from the Welsh countryside when her father changed his job. She had been ten years old at the time and never felt completely at home in the city.

The smile faded and she blinked away tears. Barely six months had passed since her mother died in a car accident, less than a year after her father suffered a fatal heart attack. The pain of their loss was still raw. Why did she have to lose everyone she loved? She swallowed hard. After the funeral, Megan discovered her mother had accumulated many debts and taken out several high-interest loans. She never mentioned money problems, and Megan had been devastated to think her mother had carried the worry herself, rather than come to her for help.

Think of the future, not the past. The money from the sale of the family home had paid off the debts and left a little over. She hoped there would be enough to allow her to give the cottage some new fittings and furniture, and a lick of paint inside and out. Since her great uncle modernised the cottage several years earlier, it was in a reasonably good state of repair and would not require too much work.

She'd managed to secure a job working as one of two receptionists for the local veterinary surgery. Although a big change from her previous high-level position as an administrator in a busy commercial office, she relished the prospect. She'd always loved animals and dealing with people. The position being mainly part-time, she would usually be finished by early or mid-afternoon. This meant there would be time to indulge her passion for painting, a passion she hoped one day to be able to make her career. On balmy summer evenings she could sit on the bench and sketch. Perhaps now she would be able to put the past behind her and instead look forward to the new possibilities this inheritance had given her. She smiled. No more business suits and severe hairstyles. No more working in a stuffy office at a monotonous, if well-paid, job. No more paying an extortionate rent for a small London flat—and no more trying to please Richard. From now on she intended to be totally independent, needing to please no-one but herself.

A faint scent of lavender drifted toward her on the warm, silky breeze. She sniffed appreciatively. It seemed a bit early for lavender, but she would have to check out the back garden once she settled in. There must be lavender bushes at the back of the cottage since she couldn't see any in the rather overgrown and neglected front garden.

She inserted the key in the door and paused. Something like the tinkle of little bells sounded close by. She looked up to see if anything in the trees could account for the sound. It might be garden chimes, but her great uncle had not been the type to have such 'fripperies' as he would have called them. She didn't think there were any other houses close enough for the sound to carry. She must be imagining things.

Megan took a deep breath and stepped into the cottage. A new home, a new job and a new beginning: A chance to put behind her the traumas of the last twelve months and start afresh.

****

Glyn Phillips, Hafod Farm, near Pentrebont, West Wales. Spring, 2023

Glyn knew there was something odd about the chestnut pony when it appeared, seemingly out of nowhere in one of his paddocks. At first, he thought she must be one of the ponies which roamed semi-wild on the mountains. They were all owned by someone and usually freeze-branded or microchipped, but this one had no owner's mark on her and his scanner revealed no microchip. Strange, and rather concerning, since they were now a legal requirement.

Unlike most of the mares on the mountain she didn't seem to be in foal, nor did she have a foal 'at foot'. So, if she had been running with one of the mountain herds, it couldn't have been for very long. She'd probably strayed when someone left a gate open, or perhaps she jumped out of her own paddock. The only way she could have got into his field was to have leapt over the fence. Although his fences were high enough to normally deter the most determined of jumpers, horses, being herd animals, would usually seek the company of their own kind. She might have managed it out of a desperate need to be with other horses.

He contacted the police, the Welsh Pony and Cob Society, the local pony club, riding club, and every horseperson on his email lists. He posted her picture on Facebook, Twitter and Instagram but no one reported losing a chestnut cob type Welsh pony mare. Nor were any of the organisations he contacted able to trace a passport or stud record relating to her. He rejected any idea of turning her out on the mountains with the wild herds in case she could not fend for herself, or in case her owner turned up looking for her.

"She's a pretty little thing, with that distinctive star on her face, but what am I going to do with her?" he said to Evan Griffith, his groom and general handyman. Evan, himself a knowledgeable horseman, backed the young ponies Glyn was too tall or heavy to ride himself.

"I can't sell her or breed from her since she doesn't legally belong to me."

"Look Glyn, why don't you just let me put a saddle on her an' let's see how she goes, like?"

Glyn frowned. "I'm not sure about that, Evan. There's no telling if she's broken to ride, although she's let me halter her and lead her around. By her teeth and general conformation, she's certainly old enough to be ridden; but she spooks at her own shadow and seems a bit temperamental."

Glyn glanced over at the mare standing in a corner of the schooling paddock. She stamped her foot and shook her head, so her long mane flowed around her like a halo, almost as if she knew they were talking about her.

"Well, she can't be any worse than some of the youngsters I've broken in for you," Evan said.

Glyn hesitated. He'd never seen a horse Evan couldn't tame, and someone had to see if she could be ridden. He knew of no one, beside Evan, light enough and competent enough to handle her if she proved difficult.

"Well, okay then. It's your choice, but make sure you wear a hard hat, I don't want to have to be visiting you in hospital." He frowned, despite his half-joking words. Evan wouldn't be happy until he tried riding the strange pony, but Glyn hoped they wouldn't regret it.

Chapter Two

The Neighbour

Apart from settling into her new job and learning the ropes, the next few weeks passed in a whirl of re-whitewashing the outside walls, hanging new curtains and painting the inside of the cottage.

Megan set up the small side room, or parlour, as a studio, with her easel, canvasses, and paints, siting a workstation in one corner for her laptop. Several old but perfectly respectable bookcases ranged along one wall, home for her collection of novels and reference books.

She paid several visits to the village Post Office in Pentrebont, which sold everything from stamps to breakfast cereal. Speaking to the chatty postmistress, she soon got to know about some of the locals. Apparently, her nearest neighbour was a Mr Phillips, a horse trainer and dealer who had bought the nearby Hafod farm about three years previously and lived there with his young son. She passed Hafod Farm on her way into the village and had noticed several horses grazing in the well-kept paddocks, so found it interesting to know who owned the place.

****

Working as a veterinary receptionist could not have been more of a change from her previous position. However, Megan soon settled in and enjoyed the work.

Although it paid less, money wasn't everything and of course she didn't have to worry about paying rent. She still had a small amount of savings put by for emergencies, so she would manage just fine, especially if her plan to sell a few paintings worked out.

The other receptionist, Mair Hughes, a girl in her mid-twenties like herself, worked full time. Mair and the two veterinary nurses, a slightly older woman, Bethan Isaac, and Catrin Jones, her own age, made her feel welcome and were happy to show her the ropes.

A special area in the small dispensary stored prescriptions, as they were made up, ready for collection. She spent some time familiarizing herself with the various names, medications and dosages. As she sorted the various prescriptions one lunchtime, she noticed a packet of anti-inflammatory and analgesic powders, with the name *Glyn Phillips, Hafod Farm,* printed on it.

"I drive past the farm on my way home, why don't I deliver this myself?" she suggested to Mair.

"Well, I was going to suggest you phone him and tell him it's ready, so he can come in to collect it, but if you're going that way you might as well just drop it off, if it's no trouble like."

"No, of course not, as I said, I have to go past the farm." Megan tucked the packet of powders into her bag so she wouldn't forget them. She'd been living at Ty Gwyn for three weeks now, it was about time she met her closest neighbour.

****

Glyn Phillips leaned over the fence of the schooling paddock, as the chestnut mare snorted and once more leapt stiff-legged high in the air. Then she exploded in a series of bone-shattering leaps and bucks with a violence which would have done justice to a rodeo bronc.

Evan had been cautious before mounting her the first time, leaning over her and not putting too much weight on her to start with. He lowered himself gently into the saddle, and at first she walked around the schooling ring with all the appearance of a quiet child's pony. Then, without warning, she sprang into a series of violent leaps and bucks for no apparent reason. This was the third time he'd got back on her.

Glyn grimaced. Evan had been insistent on trying to ride the mare, despite his misgivings. He hoped to goodness the older man would not get hurt. He half-turned at the sound of a vehicle pulling up in the yard and a car door slamming. His attention immediately turned back to the pony as, all at once, she ceased her furious bucking and stood absolutely still, eyes white-rimmed and wild, body trembling. Evan managed to leap clear a moment before the pony's legs buckled beneath her, and she lay down on her back in the sand of the schooling ring. After a minute or two, she stood again, shaking the sand off herself like a wet dog.

"Well done. That was a close one, Evan, you could have been crushed. You okay?"

"I dunno where this one came from, Glyn," Evan said, scrambling to his feet and scowling in the pony's direction, "but I reckon she's cursed. She may look like an angel when she's standin' in a field, but she's a demon when you get on her, that she is. If the devil has a horse, this must be it, you mark my words."

"Well don't take any more chances with her, Evan, I don't want to risk you getting injured."

"Don't worry, I'm not goin' to," he muttered, slapping at the dirt on his jeans with a few more choice words.

Glyn turned his head and looked behind him toward the yard, remembering the car he'd heard moments before the pony tried to roll on Glyn. A dark red SUV stood in the yard, and a young woman with long brown hair, the colour of ripe conkers and tied back in a ponytail, approached the paddocks.

He studied her with a certain amount of curiosity as she approached. They didn't get many casual visitors to Hafod, unless they were interested in discussing the purchase or training of a pony, and he had no appointments booked this evening. This unexpected caller looked like she might be rather interesting.

Chapter Three

The Demon Pony

Megan shut the gate, got back into the SUV and drove into the stable yard, glancing at the house in front of her. The large residence appeared to be built of natural Welsh stone, with a covering of ivy and Virginia creeper on the walls and around the door. Neat lawns and shrubbery surrounded the house. A newish-looking pick-up stood on the drive parked next to a large horsebox.

A range of looseboxes lined one side of the yard, and several horses grazed contentedly in the paddocks which stretched away behind the house. One of the paddocks had obviously been set aside as a nursery, where several mares stood under the trees, swishing their tails with an air of contentment, close to their long-legged foals. The fences were post and rail, well maintained, and a contrast to the barbed wire surrounding the fields of many farms in the area.

After parking and hearing voices, Megan walked across the yard toward a large open-air schooling arena adjacent to the paddocks. She was just in time to see the pony's wild display of temperament and sucked in a deep breath. Why would anyone voluntarily try to ride such a dangerous animal?

A slim, dark-haired man who looked to be in his

late twenties or early thirties, leaned over the gate of the schooling paddock. He turned his head toward her and gave her a friendly smile. She smiled back, taking in twinkling brown eyes like liquid chocolate, under a shock of dark, wavy hair and a tanned, good-looking face with a slight stubble. *Good looking* was something of an understatement. The man was gorgeous!

"Mr. Phillips? I'm from the vets. I was passing your farm, so I thought I'd drop in with this prescription for you, to save you having to pick it up in the morning," she said, handing him the package.

He tucked it into his pocket and took the hand she held out, in a firm handshake. "That's very kind of you, thank you. My old dog will be grateful if this helps ease his arthritis." He straightened up and looked back toward the schooling ring. "Excuse me for a moment, I just need to make sure Evan's all right."

"Of course," she said with a quick nod, and stood back as he opened the gate and strode across the enclosure. The short, wiry man whom Glyn Phillips called Evan, slapped the sand clinging to his jeans and muttered under his breath when Glyn reached him.

"You sure you're okay Evan?" The horse dealer's deep voice held a note of concern.

"I'll live," the other man growled, "There's not many horses get the better of me, I can tell you."

"I know—perhaps you should have talked to her in Welsh," he joked, holding the gate for the man to walk through. "It's supposed to have a soothing influence on animals."

"Little devil," Evan said, adding a few more choice swear words. "I'm bloody sure she chose the most churned up patch in the ring on purpose." He glanced across at Megan. "Sorry Miss, the little bugger—I mean beggar—got my goat she did, indeed."

She grinned at him to show she hadn't taken offence. It wasn't as if she hadn't heard worse.

"Well, you'd best go up to the house and get cleaned up while I attend to our visitor here."

Evan nodded to his boss and ambled a little stiffly toward the ivy-covered farmhouse.

Glyn Phillips turned back to Megan. "I'm very grateful to you Miss…er?"

"Johnson. Megan Johnson."

"Thank you, Miss Johnson." He slammed the gate shut and the corners of his eyes crinkled in a manner which put her at her ease and invited her to smile back. "As you say, it will save me a trip in the morning."

"It's no trouble. This place is on my way home as it happens. I'm your new neighbour." Megan looked across to the other side of the schooling ring where the mare stood, head down cropping the grass, with the reins hanging loose around her neck. "You seem to have something of a problem there though."

He frowned, his brown eyes darkening even more as he pursed his lips and followed her gaze. "Can't understand it. I never saw any pony throw Evan Griffiths three times, like she did—and make him leave a job unfinished. He's the best rider in the county—and being light and not very tall, he can usually ride any horse, big or small." He gave a wry grin. "Well, any horse except that one, anyway." He turned back to Megan. "I'd better get her unsaddled and put her back in the field with the others. I don't know what I'm going to do with her, I'm sure." He sighed deeply. "Well, it's not your problem. I'm sorry, I'm keeping you, you'll be wanting to get back home."

"Oh, it's all right, I wasn't in any hurry."

No, she wasn't in a hurry. In fact, she wouldn't have minded listening to Glyn Phillips' lyrical Welsh accent some more. He probably wouldn't appreciate her taking up his time chatting though, when he had a recalcitrant pony to catch and unsaddle, and most likely numerous other jobs needing to be done. All at once he stared past her to the paddock with a startled exclamation.

"What the…?" His face darkened, his former friendly expression changing to one of horror—fear even. He leapt over the fence with the agility of a young steeplechaser, and Megan gasped as she realised what caused the sudden change in him. A young boy, who could not have been older than about eight or nine years old, had ducked under the fence on the other side of the schooling ring. He walked calmly across the arena, leading the chestnut pony, with the air of one who knew exactly what he was doing.

The mare walked quietly beside him, her ears twitching contentedly to and fro, although Megan thought she saw something suspiciously like a gleam in her large, dark eyes.

****

Glyn stopped a few feet from the pony and slowly reached out his hand. "Huw—Huw my boy, what are you doing? Hand the reins to me, son, gently now, don't startle her."

"But Dad, she's not dangerous, she won't hurt me." So saying the boy walked straight past him toward the paddock gate. The mare followed him through, walking serenely, like a gentle riding school pony, rather than the raging little demon who had just thrown the most experienced horse breaker Glyn had ever known.

"She's fine, Dad," he said, waving a hand as he led her toward the row of looseboxes in the stable yard.

Glyn shook his head and rolled his eyes in exasperation. For a moment he'd almost forgotten his visitor. He glanced toward her and then nodded in the direction of the stables with a wry smile. "I'm sorry," he said, reluctant to appear discourteous, but desperate to make sure the boy didn't get injured. "I'd better go and make sure he's all right with that pony, please excuse me."

"Of course, I'll be on my way then. Goodnight, Mr. Phillips."

"Goodnight, Miss Johnson. Thanks again for dropping off Bob's prescription."

"No problem," she said, turning to walk back across the yard to her vehicle, with a quick wave of her hand.

Glyn sprinted toward the stables. He needed to make sure Huw didn't get hurt by the wretched pony. At the same time, he cursed himself for his abrupt dismissal of Megan Johnson. Poor woman, she must think him completely neurotic, but Huw was his only son, after all, and he couldn't help being protective.

Chapter Four

Strange Happenings

The memory of Glyn Phillips' smile stayed with Megan all the way home. The handsome, quietly spoken horse trainer she'd just met was so charismatic. He obviously doted on his son, and she could understand him being worried about him handling the wild little mare, even though she'd seemed to calm down for the boy.

She could not help wondering about the boy's mother. The village shopkeeper had informed her Glyn Phillips and his son moved into the farm about three years ago, but made no mention of anyone else. Well, it wasn't really any of her business. She would hate to be thought of as a typical 'nosy neighbour.' Still, it was difficult not to feel a bit curious.

By the time she drew up outside Ty Gwyn, the daylight had faded, and a young moon filtered through the grove of trees next to the cottage. The newly whitewashed walls which gave the cottage its name, reflected back the gentle moonlight. She couldn't help a little rush of pride. All the time and effort she'd spent on the cottage over the last weeks had been worth it!

She gave a sudden start. Was that a shadow moving in the darkened window of the kitchen? She left the car and fumbled in her bag for her keys, her hands shaking a little.

She needed to invest in a sensor light. Apart from the practicality of having such a light, she always felt a little nervous in the dark. Of course the moonlight played funny tricks sometimes, but she couldn't shake off the feeling of someone watching her. She looked around but could not make out anything suspicious in the shadows cast by the trees.

She tried to stop her hand trembling as she turned the key in the lock. She cautiously pushed open the door, wondering what she could use as a weapon if she disturbed an intruder. She swallowed hard, her heart thudding, and a slight feeling of panic rose and tightened like an elastic band around her chest. She switched on the light and gazed across the hall to the dining room. The door into the room remained closed, as she had left it. She could see no sign of anything being disturbed. She knew she hadn't left any windows open and had locked both the front and back doors securely. Logic told her no-one could have broken in without there being some sign of damage, and everything looked fine.

Ty Gwyn and the nearby village lay in a peaceful, rural area. She'd never seen anyone wandering around at night, nor felt uneasy about living there alone. The cottage being located *out in the sticks* as most people would call it, had never been a concern for her. In fact, she welcomed the peace and tranquillity after the hustle and bustle of the city. So why was she now jumping at shadows?

Taking a deep breath, she opened the dining-room door. The room looked undisturbed, everything in its usual place. The peaceful atmosphere she always felt in the cottage settled over her and she relaxed under its calming influence. She went back and double checked the locks on the doors though, just in case there were any strangers prowling around nearby.

She made herself a cup of tea and switched on the television, breathing deeply and trying to calm her nerves. After flicking through several channels, she switched it off again, finding it hard to concentrate. She did her best to dismiss the fleeting shadow she'd seen at the window, as her imagination. Gradually she settled down and let her mind wander back to Glyn Phillips and his wild pony. His rich, smoky Welsh accent kept reverberating in her mind. Hmmm, she'd better not start getting any ideas in that direction either. Her last relationship hadn't ended so well, and hadn't she vowed to avoid getting her heart bruised again?

Nothing disturbed her sleep that night, and Megan concluded the shadow she thought she'd seen was, indeed, just a trick of the moonlight.

****

The weeks flew by, and with the surgery becoming increasingly busy, Megan worked additional hours to help out. Many of the clients' pets at the surgery were isolated cases, accidents or short illnesses, but some animals needed ongoing treatment or medication. She came to know them and their owners well. She usually had weekends off and spent them, and her evenings, sketching in the garden or answering emails from friends. She'd finished giving all the rooms a new lick of paint, and with fresh new curtains and some new pieces of furniture, the place now felt like her home. The cottage still retained all its Welsh character, but looked brighter and more comfortable now, without

The Matchmaker's Mare

having lost any of its *olde worlde* charm as Megan's mother would have called it.

Pentrebont was what travel writers poetically described as 'sleepy'. The main street consisted of the Post Office and a couple of small shops, as well as the veterinary surgery and the local doctor's surgery, interspersed with little terraced houses. She found the fact the locals all talked about going to *town* rather amusing, when in England it would have been described as a small village. The nearest supermarket was five miles away, but she only bothered to shop there once a week. Most of her requirements could be bought in the village.

Although she enjoyed her work, and welcomed the extra money from the additional hours, she sometimes felt so tired she didn't feel like doing more than having an early night and reading a book in bed. On a couple of these occasions, she found the quilt turned back invitingly when she could have sworn she'd made the bed properly before leaving for work.

Once or twice she put her keys down on the little table in the hall, and when she went to fetch them, they weren't there. She would search the cottage, and when she found them, they would be on top of the refrigerator, on the table in the kitchen or somewhere else she'd not thought of looking first. She chided herself for being so absent-minded. Another time, she spent a fruitless half hour searching for her comfortable walking shoes and eventually found them in their usual place beneath the hall table. This being the first place she'd looked for them, she had no idea how she could have missed seeing them the first time. She put it down to being overtired. Perhaps she should try to get some more early nights, but she liked to make use of the longer evenings to work on her sketches and painting. The hitherto neglected garden also needed a lot of work, with spring now well underway.

She had fully expected to find at least one lavender bush to account for the delightful fragrance which occasionally wafted in on the air. She cleared most of the weeds and brambles from the garden but could see no sign of any lavender, just a few sad-looking roses. Hmm, the place did need some lavender as well as some more shrubs and bedding plants.

She took a trip to the nearest garden centre a few miles away, and purchased a few of the larger, potted lavender plants, along with some perennial shrubs and bedding plants. She would cut some lavender for the house, when it bloomed, and possibly make some little lavender-filled cushions to put in her drawers and wardrobe. Nevertheless, where the scent, which had prompted her to buy the lavender, had come from, still remained a bit of a mystery.

Working late one afternoon, a few minutes before the surgery was about to close, Megan answered the telephone and recognised the voice immediately. Deep and pleasant, soft and with a rich Welsh timbre, but not so pronounced as to make it hard to understand, there was no mistaking it. The man must have the sexiest voice in Wales.

"Glyn Phillips here. I'd just like to place an order for a repeat prescription for my dog, Bob."

"Yes, of course, Mr. Phillips, just a moment." It only took her a few seconds to find the record and check the approval. "That's fine," she said, "I'll get it made up for you, it should be ready tomorrow afternoon. I'll drop it by on my way home again, shall I?"

"No need, I can come into town tomorrow and pick it up, I don't want to put you to any trouble."

"It's no trouble at all, honestly. I have to go past your place on my way home, anyway."

"Well," he said, a slight note of hesitation in his voice, "If you're sure, Miss Johnson…"

"Of course, it's no problem. I'll see you tomorrow then." She replaced the receiver, feeling a warm glow of pleasure to think he'd remembered her name. She made a note on the database, with a little smile which she quickly suppressed. She hardly knew the man, so however nice he might seem, he was probably no different from most of the men she knew.

He could well be just another Richard—a good looking heartbreaker. Not to mention the fact he might actually have a wife somewhere, no doubt with a very good reason for not being able to be with her son and husband. She gave herself a mental slap. She should not even be thinking like this. Men were off limits, for the foreseeable future, anyway. She wasn't going to let a nice manner and fascinating, musical voice steer her away from her resolve

****

Glyn returned his mobile phone to his jeans pocket and ran the brush through the black mare's long, silky mane. It would be nice to see Megan Johnson again. How good of her to offer to deliver Bob's prescription—perhaps he hadn't made such a bad impression on her after all. He would be interested to find out how she was settling into Ty Gwyn, and whether she'd heard the rumours.

"Won't be long now, will it, old girl," he said, turning his attention back to the mare, and running a gentle hand over her swollen belly.

His mind wandered to the chestnut pony. Still no one had turned up to claim her. His intention had been to start breaking her in from scratch, spending some time with her and doing basic groundwork and long-reining. He'd hoped if he could quiet her down a bit, he could persuade Evan to try riding her again, since surely all she needed was time and patience.

However, that idea had recently been rendered unnecessary, in a way he really should have foreseen.

Chapter Five

Tea and Rumours

Golden shafts of the late afternoon sun filtered through the lush canopy of trees lining the drive to the yard at Hafod Farm.

Megan parked in front of the house, breathing in the warm, grass-scented air. Something about a balmy spring afternoon like this, made one glad to be alive. A host of birds chirped loudly in the trees, and somewhere in the distance, a pheasant made its unmistakable croaking call.

There didn't seem to be anyone around. Perhaps Glyn and his son were working with the horses in the schooling ring. Clutching the package of medication for Bob, she walked down to the paddocks and the schooling area.

She stopped in her tracks and blinked in surprise. Glyn Phillips and the stable hand, Evan Griffiths, stood as if mesmerised. The supposedly unrideable chestnut pony trotted sedately around the schooling ring with Glyn's son, Huw, on her back.

She shaded her eyes against the glare of the sun to make sure she wasn't mistaken. Glyn turned and, seeing her, beckoned her to come and stand beside him. She obliged, trying to hide her amazement while the boy cantered the pony up and down. They made a few circles and figures of eight, and then he took her over a series of small jumps situated along one side of the school. This hardly seemed like the same pony she'd watched unseat Evan a few weeks earlier.

"How on Earth did you manage to tame her?" she asked, unable to hide her admiration, not to mention her curiosity.

Glyn nodded toward her and smiled. "Afternoon, Miss Johnson. That's just it. I didn't do anything with her. The boy did it himself. I turned her out with an old mare in the bottom field, and apparently he's been going down there every morning and feeding and handling her before going to school."

Megan shot a glance at Evan Griffiths, leaning against the fence with a bemused expression on his face.

"She trusts him, see," the man said in answer to her unspoken question. "Seems like it's the only way to explain it." He paused. "P'raps she's one of those horses which prefer children to adults. Some horses do, you know."

"We only discovered Huw was riding the pony the other day, and I can't get him to tell me how long he's been riding her or how he managed to gain her confidence," Glyn added.

"Well, he seems happy," Megan replied, "and so does the pony for that matter."

The boy must have noticed her arrival and cantered up to the fence. Patting the pony's neck, he drew her to a halt and jumped down from the saddle.

"Dad, did you see me jumping?" He nodded to Megan and smiled a little shyly. "How d'you like my new pony Miss er…?" he hesitated and looked back at his father.

"This is Miss Johnson, she works at the vets. And it's your pony now, is it?" Glyn said, and Megan could not help noticing the twinkle in his eye.

His young son said nothing, but put his arm protectively around the pony's neck.

"You seem to be doing really well with her," Megan said, hastily stepping back from the fence a little, as the pony snorted and tossed her head. She turned back to Glyn. "I've brought the prescription for your dog," she said, "Would you like me to take it up to the house for you?"

"It's very kind of you, but there's no need, I don't want to hold you up."

"I'm not in any rush," she assured him. "How is he doing? Bob I mean."

"He seems to be much better, thanks. He's getting on a bit, nearly fourteen, but he's been a grand dog, and I want him to enjoy his old age as much as he can. I was afraid I might have to have him put to sleep if the medication hadn't worked. I couldn't let him carry on in pain, but it seems to have made a world of difference to the old boy." He smiled. "It's nice to think he can enjoy his twilight years. I do have a young dog as well. I've been busy with the horses lately, so Huw's been doing a lot with him, but Jack's scarcely more than a pup and still has a lot to learn."

He seemed about to say something else, but paused for a moment before asking, "Would you like to come in and see him and Bob? If you're sure you're not in a hurry, of course."

She hesitated. Was it wise to walk into someone's home when they were little more than strangers, especially somewhere so far away from other habitations? His warm smile convinced her, however. His eyes held a look of sincerity, and something about his general demeanour told her she could trust him implicitly. "Thank you," she said. "It's always nice to see how the surgery's patients are doing."

"Huw, unsaddle the pony and give her a quick rub down, then come back to the house. Supper will be ready soon."

"And I'll be off home, if there's nothing more you're needin' doing," Evan added.

"No, it's fine. I'll see you in the morning."

With a cheery wave of his hand, Evan started up his battered old van and drove off.

"And don't be long," Glyn called over his shoulder to Huw, but although his tone sounded stern, Megan noticed a grin playing at the corners of his mouth.

"No, Dad," the boy said obediently and led the mare off to one of the looseboxes.

"He'd spend all day with the horses if I let him," Glyn said, walking beside her to the house. "It's all I can do to get him to go to school in the mornings, and as soon as he comes home, he's out to the paddocks."

"Well, I reckon there are worse things he could be interested in at his age."

"You're right there. Living in the countryside there aren't a lot of things to keep a youngster interested, but he loves the outdoors. He's a good little worker and helps me no end around the stables. Thankfully he enjoys it, and though I take him for the odd trip to Carmarthen, or sometimes Cardiff, he's not really keen on the big towns and always seems to be glad to get back. I suppose you could call him a 'chip off the old block'," he added with a chuckle. When they reached the farmhouse, the door stood ajar, and Glyn stepped back a little, pushing it wider for her to enter. He walked in behind her, leaving it slightly open, letting in the still warm evening air.

Megan stepped into a large, light, and airy kitchen-cum-dining room. An Aga stove stood against one wall and bright green and white check curtains adorned the windows. Although modern, the kitchen had a rustic look and a warm, homely feel. A table and four chairs occupied the centre of the room and a couple of low, easy chairs crouched near the Aga stove. At the far end, under the window, near a small two-seater settee, a tawny long-tailed Cardiganshire Corgi curled up in one of two comfortable-looking dog beds. The dog got up, stretched, and trotted forward to greet them, wagging his tail. Megan bent to stroke his head, and he gazed up at her with large, trusting brown eyes.

"That's Bob," Glyn told her. "Jack should be around somewhere." Before he finished speaking, a black and white border collie charged through the open door and leapt toward him, whining and licking his hands. "Down boy," Glyn said, as the dog turned his attention to Megan, jumping up and almost knocking her over.

"Sorry, I do try to stop him jumping up at people, he's only young, as I said, and he gets a bit excited."

"It's okay," she said, laughing and giving the collie a hug. "I love dogs. We always had dogs when I was a child, and I really miss having one now."

"You should get one then. There are plenty in the local rehoming centre looking for a good home. I wouldn't be without a dog, myself."

"Oh, I'd love to," she said with a sigh, "but it wouldn't really be fair, since I'm at work a lot of the day. I'm thinking about getting a cat from the cat rescue centre though, although I'm really more of a dog person. Perhaps one day, if I come into money and can retire early…"

Glyn chuckled softly. "Sometimes if we want something enough we can find a way to make it happen."

Hmm, the man was a philosopher too, as well as devilishly handsome. Megan decided she would have to watch herself. A girl could find it easy to fall for his gentle manners and good looks. She gave herself a mental shake. She wasn't ready to commit to another relationship. Apart from resolving not to let herself be hurt again, she also had the satisfaction of being completely independent. To be able to organise her life to suit herself, without having to consider someone else's arrangements. Besides, she reminded himself sharply, there still remained the question of his missing wife. She'd fancied herself in love once before and had her feelings and trust betrayed. She would not allow it to happen again, or risk putting someone else's relationship in jeopardy.

Megan laid the package on the table. "Well, I'd better be going. Thanks for letting me meet your dogs." She gave both dogs a pat and turned toward the open door.

****

Damn! Glyn berated himself. He hadn't been very courteous. He'd not even offered her a cup of tea.

"Will you stay for a cup of tea, Miss Johnson, I'm just making one."

The Matchmaker's Mare

She paused. He filled the kettle and placed it on the Aga.

"Thanks, it's very kind of you," she said, turning back and sounding a trifle hesitant. "On one condition though."

"Oh, and what's that?" he asked.

"Call me Megan—you and Huw. After all, we are neighbours."

"I think we can accommodate you on that one, as long as you call me Glyn," he said with a smile.

Just then, Huw ran in and paused at the door to remove his wellington boots.

"You've brushed Seren down and given her plenty of hay and made sure she has water?"

"Yes, Dad."

"Okay then, you'd better wash your hands before supper." Huw pounded up the stairs, and Glyn poured tea into two large mugs, and a slightly smaller one.

"Please do sit down, Miss—er Megan. Milk and sugar?"

"Milk please, no sugar though," she said smiling as she sat on one of the chairs by the table.

He placed the steaming mug in front of Megan, together with a plate of biscuits.

"You called the pony *Seren*—what does it mean?" she asked, between sips.

"It's Welsh for 'Star'," he told her. "It's what the boy calls the pony. He said it's her name, as if he didn't choose it himself. He can be a strange lad sometimes. Damned if I know what to do with her," he went on. He wasn't sure why he should be sharing this particular problem with someone he'd known for such a short time, but she listened to him as if she were really interested.

"I reckon I'm going to have to let him have her unless someone turns up to claim her. He's been spending so much time with her, and she seems to have taken to him. Seems he can do anything with her, although she still won't let Evan ride her. I couldn't risk my reputation by selling her on, that's for sure, even if she were really mine to sell, which she isn't."

Megan gave him a curious look, so he explained how the mare had appeared in his paddock from nowhere, and how he'd been unable to trace her real owner. "Of course, it's always possible she's just been abandoned," he went on. "It does happen sometimes."

She gave a sympathetic nod, but didn't offer any comment, so he decided to change the subject.

"How are you settling into Ty Gwyn?"

"Fine thanks," she said. "I've more or less got it as I want it now. The garden needs some attention though."

"Well just say if you need any 'fertilizer'," he said with a grin, "I can supply as much as you want."

"Thanks," she said, smiling back. "I will."

"So everything's all right at the cottage then, you haven't been disturbed by any strange noises like?"

"Noises?" she repeated. "No," not unless you count the sound of wind chimes drifting in on the breeze, at least that's what it sounds like. Why d'you ask?"

"Oh nothing," Glyn debated whether to tell her about the rumours surrounding the cottage. He decided against it, after all they were probably just local legends, and he instantly regretted mentioning it. He wouldn't want her to be anxious or worried because of something he'd said. "I'm not sure why I said that. It's just, well you never know, you're a bit isolated there by yourself and—well forget I said anything."

Megan's expression implied she was about to ask a question, but just then Huw ran back down the stairs. "What's for supper, Dad? I'm starving."

Glyn caught Megan looking at her watch, and glancing through the window, where the sun already stained the sky in various shades of scarlet, gold, and cerise.

"I really ought to be going now. I'll leave you to have your evening meal," she said, rising from her seat.

Glyn stood and took her empty mug. He'd probably scared her away now. He wished he hadn't mentioned the cottage.

"Thanks for the tea," she said heading for the door.

"Thank *you* for dropping in the prescription," he told her. "You've saved me a trip into town."

"It's no trouble at all. I can easily drop them off whenever you need them. Goodnight Glyn—and Huw."

He stood at the open door and watched until her SUV disappeared down the lane, still annoyed with himself. She didn't look the type to be disturbed by rumours and stories. Perhaps he should have just told her the legend surrounding the cottage, after all. He sighed. Then she might have thought him a bit *touched*, and somehow, all at once, her opinion of him seemed rather important.

Chapter Six

A Stranger and a Request

Megan drove home, wondering what Glyn had meant when he talked about strange noises. She'd seen no sign of any strangers wandering about and never felt unsafe at the cottage, apart from the one time she imagined she saw a shadow at the window. Glyn had lived around there longer than her though, so perhaps it would be wise to be doubly sure she locked up and made everything secure at night, just in case.

The cottage stood cloaked in darkness when she parked in the driveway, although the daylight had not yet faded completely. The trees surrounding the house cast dark shadows, making it seem darker than it actually was. She cursed herself silently. She still hadn't got around to buying a sensor light. She fumbled in her bag for her key and turned it in the lock. Nothing happened. Strange, it had seemed all right this morning when she left for work. She tried again with the same result. Drat! It probably needed some oil. She would have to remember to pick some up in the morning on the way to work. She cursed softly under her breath and tried again. This time the door swung open, and she almost lost her balance.

"Stupid door." Megan gave herself a mental shake. No point in blaming the door, but she just hadn't expected it to open so suddenly. Remembering Glyn's words, she locked it carefully behind her. There could be no harm in being careful, although she felt sure if any strangers were wandering around, she'd have heard or seen them.

She touched the light switch and after a moment it flickered into life illuminating the diner-living room. She walked over to the windows and pulled the curtains shut, glancing at a small potted plant on the window sill as she did. "Well you look better," she breathed. The thing looked half dead when she went to water it before leaving for work, and she'd made a mental note to dispose of it when she got home in the evening. Now the small potted begonia was literally blooming, with several more buds looking ready to burst into flower.

The scent of lavender filled the room. Begonias didn't smell like that. Her brow creased in a little frown as she wondered where the scent came from. The bushes she'd planted weren't in flower yet. The pleasant fragrance, warm and spicy, reminded her of the fields of lavender in Provence she remembered from family holidays with her parents. Putting the scent out of her mind for a moment, she turned back to the begonia. Her frown turned to a half-smile, pleased it had survived, and she hadn't killed it by neglect. Its almost miraculous recovery was a bit of a mystery though. She must be a better gardener than she'd believed.

While she prepared her evening meal her thoughts kept turning back to Glyn Phillips, wondering what happened to his wife. Perhaps she would make some discreet enquiries, just out of neighbourly interest of course.

****

Several weeks passed before Megan brought up the subject as casually as she could while having lunch with Mair and the two veterinary nurses.

"Glyn Phillips' son is getting on well with his new pony," she said, trying to sound offhand and biting into a wholemeal egg and cress sandwich. "According to Glyn—er—Mr. Phillips, no one else can ride the pony except the boy, not even his stableman, Evan Griffiths."

Bethan looked up from her mug of hot chocolate—even in the middle of summer, all she drank was hot chocolate. "You've been over at the Phillips' farm quite a lot lately, haven't you?" she observed with a grin.

"Well," she said, trying to sound non-committal, "I have to go past the farm on my way home, so it makes sense to drop off his prescriptions and the special dog food we supply for Bob. It saves him the bother of having to drive in for them himself."

She could not deny she looked forward to those visits. Dropping off any prescriptions or dog food, or sometimes wormers or vitamin supplements for the horses on her way home was no trouble. When she had nothing to deliver and no reason for visiting, it almost felt as if something was missing. She had fallen into the habit of stopping for a short while on her way home if she happened to spot Glyn or Huw in the yard. She would enquire about Bob or ask how Huw was doing at school, just by way of being neighbourly of course, but she always enjoyed these brief chats.

"He's quite a 'hottie', isn't he though," Catrin put in, winking, and then blushing deep pink. "If I didn't have a boyfriend…" she hesitated for a moment. "I'm quite surprised he hasn't been snatched up by now.

After all, it's been about three years since he bought Ty Gwyn and he's such a catch—"

"What happened to Huw's mother?" Megan enquired, wiping her mouth with a paper serviette and taking a sip of tea, pleased Catrin had brought up the subject of Glyn's eligibility. She did not want to sound too interested in the handsome horse trainer herself. "I mean, are they divorced or something?" Then, realising this might still seem a little too inquisitive, she added quickly, "It seems a shame for a young lad like that to be growing up without a mother"

"They say she ran off with a man from the Midlands," Mair said. "Just upped and left with him she did, before Mr Phillips moved here."

"We don't know that for sure," Bethan stated. "You're only going by what old befuddled Mary said when she brought her cat in that time, Mair. It could be just plain old gossip, you know how things get exaggerated in a place like this." She turned to Megan and lowered her voice conspiratorially. "We know he came from somewhere down south in the valleys, before he bought Hafod Farm, but no one seems to know much about him. He's always very friendly when he comes into the surgery, but he never talks about himself."

"Well, if she did leave him, all I can say is 'stupid woman'," Catrin said darkly. "I wouldn't have left a man like Glyn, or a lovely little boy like Huw. Some people just don't know when they're well off, they don't."

Bethan frowned at her over her mug of chocolate. "As I said, we don't know for sure she left him. For all we know, his wife could've died of a terminal illness, or a tragic accident, and he's moved here to forget."

"P'raps that's why he's never hooked up with anyone else. He has a broken heart poor dab," Catrin said in dramatic tones.

"Or perhaps the rumours *are* true, or they just didn't get on and are divorced and he's been put off women forever," Mair told her, taking a large bite out of a cream doughnut. "Honest, Catrin, you read too many romances, you do."

"Well, in every romance I read there's always a happy ending, so I just hope there's someone out there to mend his heart," Catrin retorted.

Megan said nothing but smiled and changed the subject. After all, this was merely conjecture, and she was still not much wiser about Glyn Phillips. He could be widowed, divorced—or still married, with a secret, deranged wife hidden away somewhere, like Mr. Rochester in *Jane Eyre*.

****

Megan checked the appointments for the morning and looked up when the doorbell chimed and a tall, extremely good-looking young man with blond hair and a self-confident air, walked up to the counter.

She tried not to stare—he was one of the most striking men she'd ever seen.

With wavy, sandy hair, piercing green eyes and a firm, square jaw, he had the self-assured air of someone well aware of the effect he had on women. Impeccably dressed, from his dark blue suit to his glossy, expensive-looking shoes, he might have stepped straight off a film set.

"Good morning," he said flashing a broad smile, and she caught the heady aroma of expensive aftershave. "Is Bethan in today?"

"Just a moment," Megan said, aware he seemed to be studying her intently and hoping she wasn't blushing. She scanned the details on the screen in front of her. "She's assisting with an operation at the moment," she told him with an apologetic smile. "Is there anything I can help you with? Do you have an appointment?" She noticed he did not have an animal of any sort with him, but perhaps he just wanted something routine. Maybe a canine nail clipping and he'd left the dog in his car while he checked whether Bethan would be able to attend to it. That would be a little unusual, because normally clients just checked in at reception rather than requesting a particular nurse.

"No, it's fine, thank you," he said. "Just be a love and tell her Mark called in, would you?"

"Yes, of course I will, is there any other message?"

"No, that's all. It's not anything urgent. I can pop in later."

So, this was a social call, rather than a veterinary visit. Perhaps Mark was Bethan's boyfriend. He certainly knew how to make an impression, even if he did seem a bit too sure of himself. Perhaps he had a right to be, looking the way he did. He paused at the door, with a wave of his hand.

Just then the telephone rang. She nodded goodbye and listened attentively to the woman at the end of the phone, going on in great detail about her beloved cockapoo's rather unfortunate gastric condition. When she could get a word in edgeways, she suggested she make an appointment to bring the dog in to be examined by one of the vets and have the appropriate treatment administered.

Later the same morning, when Bethan had finished assisting with the operation and they sat in the restroom enjoying a cup of tea, she passed on the message.

"Someone called Mark came by asking for you," she said, trying to keep the curiosity out of her voice.

"Oh yes," Bethan said cheerily. "He's my brother. He often pops by here, and we go out for a bit of lunch together. I'll send him a text and catch up with him later."

Ah, that explained it. The resemblance became apparent now she knew the relationship. She wondered why she had not seen it before. Bethan had similar wavy sandy coloured hair and green eyes, as well as being attractive and having the same air of self-assurance as her brother.

Over the next couple of weeks Mark often called into the office and always took time to chat to Megan. He took notice when she was particularly busy though and kept his comments brief at such times. However, when no one sat in the waiting area, he'd engage her in conversation and crack jokes, and she had no doubt he'd been flirting with her. Of course, Bethan teased her unmercifully.

"I think my brother is keen on you, Megan, girl," she said half-jokingly one day at lunch. "I warn you though, he can be a bit of a lady killer, and he changes his women as often as he changes his socks, he does."

"Don't worry," Megan said with a dismissive smile, "I'm sure there are a lot of women out there he'd fancy more than me, and I'm really not interested in men at the moment. No disrespect to Mark, of course, he looks quite a catch," she added hastily, afraid she might have offended the other woman. Bethan just grinned, and tapped her nose, as if to say she knew something Megan didn't.

After her shift, she said goodbye to the girls, deciding to spend the rest of the afternoon painting. She took her easel and paints down to the river and set up near the footpath.

She breathed in the faint scent of horses borne on the slight breeze, mingling with the fresh aroma of grass, letting her mind wander to her innermost dreams. She longed to someday be able to make her living from painting. She'd graduated with a good Honours degree in fine art but had never been able to find the time she needed to commit fully to the occupation she loved. She'd been intent on paying off her mother's debts after her death and needed to know she had a steady income to keep herself fed and to pay the bills. Perhaps one day she would be able to devote more time to work on achieving her dream. In the meantime, she intended to make the most of every opportunity to indulge in her passion.

She studied the trees overlooking the water, the sun sparkling off the surface, and the trees bending low, leaves reflected in the crystal-clear water. Small families of ducks and ducklings glided by on the water, looking for food, and the occasional jewel-bright flash of incandescent blue signalled a kingfisher diving for fish. The river ran alongside Glyn's fields, and she often caught the glimpse of a shiny brown or chestnut flank through the hedge. The only sound disturbing the silence, apart from the twittering of birds, was the occasional low snort or whinny, or an impatient stamp of a hoof on grass.

After making some quick, pencil sketches, and a

charcoal outline, she proceeded to paint. Clear blue for the sky, the wisps of white cloud, tinged with silver, drifting across. The leaves of the trees varied in shades of green, from pale and delicate, to dark, almost black, in the shadows.

By the time she finished for the day, the sun had sunk in the sky, turning the white fluffy clouds overhead to crimson, pink, and peach, although the light was still good. She stepped back and looked appraisingly at the painting. Hmm, not too bad. She could finish touching up when she got home. Maybe she would paint another aspect of the river tomorrow. She packed away her equipment, leaving the painting on the easel to finish drying, and became aware she was not alone.

****

Glyn put his fingers to his mouth and whistled, but the two dogs bounded up behind Megan, for once completely ignoring him, winding themselves around her legs. She turned and knelt to stroke them, the scent of wet dog tickling her nose.

"Whoa, steady boys. Hello Bob, you're looking good—and Jack," Megan added, cuddling the two dogs, and laughing as they tried to lick her face.

"Hi, Glyn," she said, standing and turning when he reached her.

"I hope they didn't startle you, too much, or get you wet—I'm afraid they've been paddling in the river."

"No, it's fine, these are only my old jeans." She stood back while Glyn stood admiring the painting on the easel.

"I didn't know you could paint."

"It's very relaxing," she said, sounding a little self-conscious. "I hadn't expected to see anyone here, it seemed pretty deserted. I've only seen one or two walkers all afternoon."

"I often walk along the riverside with the dogs," he told her. "I didn't know you came here too, though. I have to say it seems a perfect place to paint."

"It is, isn't it?" she agreed.

He scrutinised the painting. He was no expert but could see the skill in the work. "This is really good, do you paint professionally?"

"Well, I don't think I could call myself a *professional*. I've sold a few paintings, although I'm not sure I could make my living from it at the moment, which is why I work part-time at the vets."

She smiled, in the way she had that seemed to light up her face. "I do need to have a regular income to pay the bills. It's something I really enjoy though, and I'd love to be able to make it my full-time job one day."

"Do you just paint landscapes?"

"No, I do portraits, and animals too, sometimes."

"Would you do one for me?" he asked. "It would be great to have a painting of Huw and that pony of his."

"Of course, I'd love to," she said. She took down the painting and carefully placed it in her case.

"Wonderful, and of course I'll pay you the going rate."

"What? Oh no, I couldn't take any payment, I'll enjoy doing it—"

"I insist, after all, it's your time and materials." No way would he expect her to do it for nothing. He gave what he hoped was a persuasive smile. "How will you ever be able to make it your living if you don't charge people for your work?"

She smiled back. "All right then, but *mates' rates*—okay?"

He hesitated for a second. "If you insist, although I'd prefer to pay you the full price."

"When would you like me to start?"

"Well, when you can, but I don't want to rush you if you're busy…"

She shook her head. "No, it's fine. I'd need to know what sort of size you want and things like that though."

"Of course. Will you need him to stand still for you? I'm not sure how long he'd be able to manage that, she's quite a fidgety pony."

"No problem," she said as she finished gathering up her painting materials and packed them away in their containers. "As long as I can get some good sketches, I should be able to make a passable likeness, and some photographs would help, if you have them. In fact, it might be nice to get an action painting of him jumping, don't you think?"

"That sounds like a great idea" he told her. "I took quite a few shots of him on my phone while he was practising jumping the other day, I'll sort some out for you and get them printed off—or I can put them on a memory stick if that would be better."

"Sounds good, I'm looking forward to it already."

"I'll pop over with them later if it's all right with you, and I'll measure up the space where I decide to hang it, so you'll know what size."

They walked over to where she'd left her SUV, and he helped her load the easel and painting materials into the back, before saying their goodbyes.

He walked home to the farm with the dogs and whistled softly to himself, excited at the prospect of having an original painting of Huw.

If he was honest with himself, though, he looked forward to the prospect of spending more time with Megan even more.

Chapter Seven

The Legend

True to his word, Glyn called at the cottage later the same evening. "Sorry to call round late, but I had a few things to do. I've left Huw at home doing his homework."

"That's all right, Megan said, smiling. "It's only just gone eight, and I wasn't going out or anything. Come on in." She set a mug of tea before Glyn, and he laid an assortment of printed photographs on the table in front of her. He'd also transferred some others to a memory stick as promised, and she inserted it into her laptop.

"I hope these are what you wanted. I can get you some more if you need them."

There were several photographs of Huw and the chestnut pony standing. Most of the pictures showed him and the mare clearing a variety of small fences, though, and those were the ones Megan studied hardest. An action painting would be more interesting.

"They're perfect. I can do the preliminary sketches from these, and then I'll come along to the farm and do some from life, as it were."

"Great. When do you think you can start?"

"Well, we're pretty busy at the surgery at the moment, and I may have to do some extra shifts, but I'll try and work on the sketches when I'm home and give you a call one afternoon next week, to arrange coming over."

"That would be grand, and you don't have to worry about calling me, it's not often I'm not at home. Any time you can make it after Huw gets home from school, at about a quarter past four, will be fine."

"Okay then, as soon as I get those first sketches done, I'll pop over."

He set down his now empty mug. "Thanks for the tea. I'd best be off, I don't want to leave Huw by himself too long. He's big enough to look after himself for a bit, and he has the dogs, but I can't help worrying, if I have to leave him, and it'll be his bedtime soon."

"Of course. I'll see you next week then."

Glyn rose to leave, and a sharp breeze blew in through the slightly open window, bringing with it the now familiar scent of lavender. The photographs fluttered off the table, where he'd laid them out so carefully when he arrived. He and Megan bent down together and as they gathered up the prints, their hands touched. A tingling sensation shot through her like an electric shock, causing her blood to heat and her breath to catch.

They stood quickly, and both laughed somewhat nervously. She glanced at his face and felt herself flush. She had the feeling he too, was a little embarrassed. For a fleeting moment, she wondered if he'd felt the same jolt of electricity she had, then pushed the thought aside. She needed to stop acting like an infatuated schoolgirl.

He took the photos and placed them in a neat pile back on the table.

"I'll see you out," she said, quickly shutting the window. "It's getting breezy all at once, I hope the weather isn't about to change."

She saw him to the door, already looking forward to her visit to the farm next week. She could have sworn she heard a soft chuckle—and that scent of lavender again. She shrugged her shoulders, Strange how the imagination could play tricks in these old houses. Just as well she didn't believe in the supernatural.

****

Although Megan enjoyed her work at the surgery, she looked forward to her free time when she could work on the sketches of Huw and his pony. She'd needed to work over, once or twice, but she'd completed her preliminary pencil sketches and watercolours. She was now ready to add the finishing touches from life before she started the actual painting on canvas.

She worked on variations over the weekend and could hardly wait to take the final sketches over to Hafod Farm, to see what Glyn thought of them.

She drew up in the yard, inhaling the now familiar and not unpleasant horse and stable aromas, to be greeted by the two dogs. "Hello Jack, hello Bob, old chap," she said, smiling at Glyn as he walked toward her. She took her sketchpad and portfolio out of the car and showed the sketches to him.

"I've done a couple of watercolours," she said, "but I want to do the main painting in acrylics."

"Acrylics? Don't you use oils?"

She shook her head. "I find acrylics easier to work with. They dry more quickly, too."

He laughed. "Just shows how much I know about painting."

"What do you think of these sketches, are they anywhere near what you had in mind?"

"They're amazing. You really are talented. I'm no artist myself, but they tell me horses are quite difficult to draw."

"Well, it helps to know the bone and muscle structure," she said, feeling a little thrill of pleasure at the compliment. She was not a vain person, but the praise felt good. Richard had always dismissed her painting as 'your little hobby' and never given her any real encouragement. "I've had to do quite a lot of research," she went on. "Luckily there were several reference books I could borrow from the vets, and your photos helped, too. I want to watch Huw and Seren jump again though, so I can see how the muscles move under the skin, and how the light strikes the pony's coat—things like that."

Glyn nodded, and they walked over to the schooling ring together, to see Huw already taking Seren over a set of small fences.

****

An hour or so later, she laid her sketchpad in the back of her SUV.

"Let me see," Huw begged, slipping off the pony and holding her bridle reins in one hand, while he hopped excitedly around on one foot.

Megan laughed at his keenness, and he handed Seren's reins to his father, standing close to Megan while she showed them some of the sketches. "These are only rough drafts. It'll be a week or two before I finish the proper painting."

"Aw," Huw said, "I thought you'd have it done by tomorrow."

She smiled. "Sorry, Huw, it'll take a little longer than that. You'll just have to be patient."

"You heard what Megan said," Glyn told him. "Now get along with you. Rub Seren down well before you turn her out."

He turned to Megan and grinned. "I can't say I blame him. I'm dying to see the finished painting myself."

"You'll just have to be patient," she repeated, smiling to show she wasn't serious. "I'd rather you didn't see it until it's quite finished."

"All right, you win. Now suppose you come up to the house for a cup of tea? You don't have to get back yet do you?"

She nodded. "Thanks, I have to admit I could do with a cuppa now." They walked up to the house together, and Megan stretched out in one of the comfortable chairs while Glyn busied himself making a brew.

She accepted the steaming mug gratefully. "Why don't you and Huw come over to Ty Gwyn one evening for supper, when I've finished the painting?"

"That sounds wonderful, Megan. We'll look forward to it, thank you."

Driving back to Ty Gwyn, Megan hummed softly to herself, with a happy feeling of anticipation. Once she arrived at the house, she took her sketching materials from the SUV and carried them into the kitchen. She laid the sketches out on the kitchen table and studied them with a certain amount of satisfaction.

She had spotted a little picture framing shop in the

village and decided once she finished the painting, she would get the picture framed for Glyn as a surprise. She would charge him for the painting, as agreed, but the frame would be a little extra gift, from her.

Besides the sketches of Huw and the pony, there were some more drawings which she hadn't shown Glyn. They were of Glyn himself, drawn from memory, and she smiled as she studied them. Yes, she really seemed to have captured the likeness well, the dark, wavy hair, strong jawline and the gentle expression on his face and in his eyes. Even though they were only black and white sketches she was well pleased with them. They, and the sketches of Huw and Seren were some of her best work. She put them carefully away in a drawer. She wouldn't show them to Glyn, at least not yet. They would be her secret. She might surprise him with them some day, if she could pluck up the courage. She could not help wondering what he would say if he knew she'd been sketching him without his knowledge.

He'd be flattered Megan, You know he would. Why don't you show them to him?

There was that voice in her head again. Was she going crazy? Or was her subconscious trying to tell her something—the fact her feelings for Glyn were now bordering on infatuation? She shook her head, annoyed at herself. Of course they weren't. She and Glyn were friends, nothing more. One day, perhaps, she might let him see the sketches. For now, they stayed in the drawer.

****

Several weeks later

Megan laid the table in the dining room for three and set a small glass vase of deep pink roses from the garden as a centrepiece. They made a pretty splash of colour against the crisp white tablecloth, and she allowed herself a quick smile of satisfaction.

An aroma of roast chicken and herbs permeated the kitchen. She would serve it with fresh vegetables from her garden, and roast potatoes, and she had some non-alcoholic fruit wine chilling in the fridge. Huw would be able to enjoy a drink with the adults, and not feel left out.

For dessert she'd prepared a fresh fruit compote to be accompanied by home-made vanilla ice cream. Simple fare, nothing complicated, but she had a feeling Glyn appreciated good, wholesome home cooking. Anyway, much as she enjoyed cooking, she did not want to risk anything too ambitious, in case it did not turn out quite as she'd intended, or even worse, was a complete disaster.

The doorbell chimed at exactly seven o'clock. Well, Glyn was certainly punctual. As the musical chimes ran out and she hurried to open the door, she noticed how they had an after-sound, like little bells. Strange, she hadn't noticed it before, perhaps it was just an echo.

Both Glyn and Huw looked very smart. Glyn wore fawn slacks and a bright blue open-necked shirt, and she caught a subtle whiff of aftershave, although not nearly as strong as the one Mark always wore. Huw, dressed in dark trousers and a casual check shirt, and looking a little shy, handed her a large bunch of carnations and oriental lilies.

"Oh, thank you, they're beautiful. How kind of you. Come on in, both of you, don't stand out there on the doorstep."

She showed them into the dining room. "Would you like something to drink before we start? Dinner won't be long, I just have to dish it out."

"No, we're fine thanks," Glyn said. "Can we do anything to help?"

Megan smiled. "No, it's all under control, thanks. Just make yourselves comfortable." She went into the kitchen and filled a vase with water for the flowers before snipping the ends off the stems and arranging them. She placed the vase of flowers on the sideboard in the dining room then went back to fetch the wine and check the chicken. Crisp and golden on the outside, it also gave off a delicious aroma and would soon be ready to serve.

She had prepared fresh melon boats for starters, and when she took them into the dining room, Huw and Glyn polished them off in no time. The main course and sweet also seemed to go down well, to her relief. After they finished, Glyn and Huw both said how much they'd enjoyed the meal.

Glyn insisted on helping her carry the plates and dishes into the kitchen. "That was delicious," he said, "let me help you with the washing up."

Megan grinned. "No need, just leave them there on the worktop. I have one of those modern, new-fangled things called a *dishwasher* now."

"Hm, I might have to invest in one of those myself," Glyn said, "they must save a fair bit of time."

"They do," she agreed, walking back with him into the living room.

"Did you finish the painting?" he asked. "I can't wait to see it."

"Oh yes, of course." Megan had purposely waited

until after dinner, half excited to show it off, and half nervous in case it didn't meet his expectations.

She went over to the corner and picked up a brown paper package which she handed to Glyn. "I do hope you like it." She'd not only finished the painting, but had it framed, once the varnish was dry.

Glyn unwrapped it with great care, and gave a gasp of admiration, while Huw jumped up and down with excitement.

The pony leapt over the fence, half facing the observer, so Huw's face was visible too, and she'd managed to capture the delight on the boy's face.

"It's beautiful," Glyn told her, and Megan felt her cheeks flush with pleasure.

"It's so vivid I feel I can almost hear the pony snorting, he went on, "You've managed to portray Seren and Huw very realistically, while not losing the effect of a painting. It's stunning, isn't it Huw?"

"I really, really love it," Huw said, leaning over his shoulder to have a closer look. "I didn't know you could paint like that, Megan. I wish I could draw horses."

Her cheeks flushed again. "Thank you. I'm so glad you're both pleased with it." She glanced at Huw. "Horses are quite hard to draw properly, but there are one or two tricks to make it a bit easier. I'll show you tomorrow, after work, if you like."

"Oh yes, please." Huw gazed at her with something like awe, and Glyn also looked at her as if she'd just announced she could walk on water.

"I'll brew some tea," she said quickly, feeling rather shy, under Glyn's admiring gaze. "Unless you would prefer coffee," she said, nodding toward him.

"No, tea's fine for us both," Glyn assured her.

She slipped into the kitchen and came back a few minutes later with a tray, three mugs and a plate of shortbread biscuits and chocolate cupcakes she'd baked that afternoon. She'd discerned Huw shared her love of chocolate, and Glyn seemed to enjoy it as well.

"I'm not sure I could eat anything more after that wonderful meal," he said with a wink.

"Well, perhaps you could manage a shortbread?" she suggested, as Huw happily helped himself to one of the cupcakes.

"They do look tempting," Glyn admitted, taking one and smiling appreciatively. They chatted about painting and Huw's schoolwork and pony for a while, and he again complimented Megan on the painting. Then he glanced around the room and gave her a very direct look.

"How are you enjoying living here?" he asked. "You seem to have made this old cottage very cosy and comfortable."

"Oh yes, I love it," she told him. "I wouldn't go back to the city if you paid me."

He grinned. "That's good." Then all at once, he looked serious. "You've not had any problems, strange noises or anything?"

She frowned wondering what he was getting at. This was the second time he'd mentioned strange noises. "No, not really. Nothing I wouldn't expect from a cottage this old anyway. She studied his face, her curiosity aroused. "You asked me that before, is there something about this cottage you're not telling me?"

****

Glyn glanced away for a moment, feeling slightly

sheepish. Was she going to think him completely mad? Why had he brought this up again? Well, there was no help for it. He'd better finish what he'd started. "As you probably know, there are a lot of old myths and legends in these parts. Wales is steeped in them, actually. One concerns a young woman called Rhiannon, who lived in this cottage long ago."

"Go on," she prompted, seeing him hesitate once more.

"Well, apparently, as well as being the village matchmaker, she also cared for all the sick and injured animals the villagers brought her. She loved animals and especially, her little mare, which the villagers whispered, had the power of flight. Others said this was just a rumour put about by folk with an overactive imagination."

"So what happened to her?" she asked.

"Sion Sienco, a local gypsy, was forever playing tricks on Rhiannon to try to gain her attention, but to start with she would have nothing to do with him. Sion had a little white magic and would do things like causing her milk cow to go dry or spiriting away her beloved pony and hiding the animal in the woods."

She grinned at him over the rim of her mug. "I'm not surprised she spurned his advances if he did things like that."

He smiled ruefully. "I suppose men sometimes do silly things when they're in love, and of course it happened a very long time ago, and stories become distorted in the telling. If there's any truth in it at all, of course."

"Well, what happened then," she asked, sounding really interested. "Did they ever get together, in the end?"

"It's rather a sad story actually." Glyn set down his mug carefully. "They both died tragically young."

"Oh no, how awful..." her voice trailed off, her expression downcast.

"Eventually he won her over," Glyn went on, "and they planned to get married. Her father had other ideas, though, and arranged for her to marry a rich landowner, who besides being cruel, was also a mage. She and Sion fled in the night. They rode for several days, but the mage caught up with them in a snowstorm. They'd ridden up a treacherous mountainside, a good many miles from here, *Mynydd y Graig*, known in English as the Dragon Mountain. He and the gypsy fought, but despite Sion having some magic himself, he was no match for the dark arts practised by the mage. The story goes he overcame Sion and slew him with a poison-tipped sword."

He paused for a moment, seeing Megan's face become even more concerned. "Rhiannon, overcome with grief, threw herself at the mage, in an attempt to disarm him and kill him with his own sword, but he flung her violently to the ground. Her faithful pony lashed out at him with both her hind hooves and caught him off-guard. He stepped too close to the edge in an effort to get away from the enraged animal, slipped over, and tumbled down the mountainside, causing a landslide which buried him forever."

"Served him right—but what a sad story," Megan said, with a catch in her voice. "What happened to Rhiannon?"

"According to the legend, she sat with Sion in her arms while the snow fell, covering them both. She died of cold and a broken heart, holding him there on the mountainside. Although Sion's gelding and the mage's stallion made it back down the mountainside, Rhiannon's mare was never seen again. Some say she refused to leave her mistress and died there with her, in the snow."

Megan looked so sad Glyn immediately regretted telling her the story. He fought the urge to reach out and put his arms around her. Instead, he said, "I'm sorry, I didn't mean to upset you. It's only a story, you know."

She remained silent for a moment. "No, it's all right. It's such a tragic tale, though. I suppose you're going to tell me Megan haunts this cottage, now."

He smiled a little hesitantly. "That's what they say—and Sion as well. According to the legend, Rhiannon's father was wracked with remorse for the rest of his life and died a few years later. After his death, Sion and Rhiannon's spirits returned to the cottage. Of course, as I said, it's only an old folk tale."

"Nevertheless," Megan said, pursing her lips, "these legends usually have some basis in fact."

"You have a point there," he replied. "In those days girls were often forced to marry a man of their father's choosing, although of course her *intended* is unlikely to have been an actual mage. Perhaps he did murder Sion in revenge for him running away with Rhiannon, and the magical element was later added to make the story more interesting." He paused again. "I hope I haven't made you feel nervous or anything. You don't believe in ghosts, do you?"

"Of course not. It takes more than an old legend to scare me. Anyway, if she and Sion do haunt this cottage, I've never felt in danger here, or a sense of anything—anything sinister or unearthly."

Glyn smiled again. "Well, there probably isn't much left of the original cottage anyway. It must have been rebuilt and extended several times over the years, although I expect the stone walls are the same. As for the spirits, I don't think they're supposed to be dangerous, or even in the least bit threatening, and of course, there aren't really any such things as ghosts. I thought I ought to warn you though, just in case you heard the rumours from someone else and were worried."

Megan shook her head. "No, I'm not worried—and my uncle never said anything about the cottage being haunted. Mind you, he probably wouldn't have believed it if a ghost had stepped out in front of him. Great Uncle Thomas was very down to earth."

"Good. That's all right then." He glanced at his watch. "It's getting late, and this young man ought to be in bed," he said, glancing down at the boy.

"Of course," she agreed as Glyn rose and gently pulled Huw to his feet. "Thank you so much for coming, it's been a lovely evening."

He took the carefully wrapped, precious painting and placed it under his arm.

"We've enjoyed it very much," he told her. "Haven't we Huw?"

"Yes, thank you very much," Huw said, looking up at Megan, with a happy grin on his face.

"I've loved having you." She ruffled his hair gently as she saw them to the door.

"Thank you so much again for the wonderful meal—and the beautiful painting—and for getting it framed," Glyn said, hoping she realized how much he appreciated it. "The frame is so elegant and just right for the painting, I wasn't expecting you to do that as well. How much do I owe you for it?"

She shook her head, "Nothing, consider it a gift. You've paid me for the painting, and I thought it would be nice to have it mounted for you."

For a moment, Glyn was lost for words. "It's really kind of you," he said after a brief pause. "I don't know how to thank you."

"No need," she said quickly. "I'm just happy you like it."

"It's perfect." He turned back, as Huw trotted ahead to the car, and placed a hand lightly on her arm. She looked so lovely, standing there in the doorway, the moonlight catching her hair and giving it a coppery sheen. He stifled the urge to take her in his arms and kiss her. Now was not the time.

"See you tomorrow then?"

A soft breeze seemed to come from nowhere, carrying with it the scent of lavender.

"Yes, of course, We're a bit busy, but I'm hoping I won't have to work too late."

He smiled and turned to follow Huw with a wave of his hand, wondering what her lips would have tasted like if he *had* kissed her goodnight.

Chapter Eight

An Invitation

A soft wisp of something like smoke, or early evening mist, drifted near the vase of flowers in the dining room. Slowly the mist formed itself into the shape of a young woman in a flowing, diaphanous gown. The figure flickered and gradually solidified.

"What did I tell you, Sion? Was I not right? Do you not agree those two make a perfect match?"

A similar wisp of mist, wavered and swirled, to become a handsome young man in a laced up shirt and breeches. He seated himself opposite her and crossed his long legs.

"If you say so, Rhiannon, cariad, just don't get me involved in your matchmakin' schemes."

"Well, if I need your help with this one, do not forget you owe me, Sion Sienco. I have not yet forgiven you for taking my pony and having me search half the day to find out where you left her, even if it did help bring those two together. I will not let you get away with it."

****

The next day passed quickly and despite being busy, Megan's thoughts kept returning to Glyn. He'd said he would hang the painting of Huw and his pony above the fireplace in their front room, and she couldn't help a small thrill of pride. It had turned out better even than she'd hoped, and the fact Glyn seemed so pleased with it lifted both her spirits and her confidence.

She'd remembered her promise to Huw and slipped her sketchbook and pencils into the glove compartment before setting off for work. As soon as she drove into the yard, Huw came running up. The way he always seemed so happy to see her was rather touching.

"Hello, Megan," he began, when she opened the door, his voice full of excitement. "Are you going to teach me how to draw horses today?"

"Yes," just give me chance to get out of the car," she said, laughing. "Where's your dad?" she asked, looking around.

"Oh, he's over at the stables I think," he said. "He waited around for a bit, but you're later than you usually are, so he had to do the evening feeds. Can we start now—can we?"

Megan couldn't help smiling at his enthusiasm. They sat at the picnic table outside the house, and she showed him how to start drawing with simple ovals and lines, taking care to get the proportions right. Then she explained how to gradually sketch in the correct shape, shading in the original pencil lines to give an indication of texture and lighting. Huw showed himself to be a good pupil and learnt quickly, showing real keenness and more talent than she'd expected for a boy his age.

While he drew, he chatted about Seren and how he was training her, and what he'd learned at school. Then he showed her an essay he had written, entitled *What I want to do in the holidays*. He described how he intended to continue the training of his pony during the summer break, and the way he took care of her. To

Megan's surprise, she was mentioned as well. She found it rather flattering to be included, even if just the information she worked at the vets and delivered Bob's food and medication. He also described how she'd painted a picture of him and his pony.

She helped him with one or two grammatical and spelling errors and handed back the essay. "It's very good, Huw. You should get good marks." He beamed with pleasure. Then Megan spotted Glyn striding across the yard toward them, and Huw ran up to him to show him his drawing.

After making some complimentary remarks, Glyn nodded in her direction.

"Evening, Megan, I was getting a bit worried, you're not usually this late."

"Sorry," she called out as she unlocked the back of her vehicle and hauled out a couple of large sacks of dog food. "I got held up."

"You don't need to apologise to me, *cariad*, but don't tell me they made you work late again," Glyn said. He took the bags off her and stacked them in the shed. "I know it's none of my business, but don't you think you're a bit too easy-going? You always seem to be working extra hours there."

"No, not this time, and anyway I never mind working over, I love working at the vets. No, it wasn't that." she hesitated. Should she tell him Mark had come in just as she was about to leave and again asked her if she'd go out with him. Glyn gave her a questioning look, and she knew there was no point in trying to fob him off. They were getting to know each other too well to hide things.

"As a matter of fact, one of the veterinary nurses

has a brother who is keen to take me out on a date." She paused. "I didn't have to work late, but he called in just as I was leaving and kept me talking."

Glyn raised an eyebrow. "Oh, yes?" His voice betrayed nothing, but he seemed to stiffen a little and did not look at her as he spoke. Megan waited for him to ask if she'd accepted, but he didn't, merely shutting the feed shed door after tipping the dog food into a vermin-proof bin. For some reason, she felt she ought to say something to lighten the mood. "He can be a bit persistent. I had to use delivering your dog food as an excuse to put off giving him an answer tonight." She grinned. "You know I sometimes think the matchmaking ghost you were telling me about is trying to get me paired up. It's the third time Mark's asked me in a fortnight."

"Really?" He nodded in the direction of the house. "Coming up for a cup of tea?"

"I'd love to, thank you," Megan said with a smile, relieved he hadn't pursued her comment further.

****

Megan sat in the comfortable kitchen, sipping the Earl Grey he'd just made, and Glyn noticed her looking through the window, as Huw brought Seren into the stable yard. The kitchen had a good view of the stables, and she watched Huw brush the pony and pick up her feet to clean out her hooves, before taking her into her loosebox.

She turned back to him. "Huw looks after the pony well, doesn't he!"

Glyn nodded, unable to hide his pride in his young son. "He's a natural. I've always impressed on him that if you have animals they have to be cared for, and he knows however tired or hungry he is himself, the pony's welfare comes first."

Megan took a bite out of a chocolate digestive biscuit and another sip of her tea as Glyn came and sat opposite her. "I was thinking, it's Saturday tomorrow, so I'm guessing you'll be having the day off, so why don't the three of us go for a ride? This is lovely riding country, especially at this time of year, and I'm sure I must have a horse to suit you." He turned to look at her. "You do ride, don't you?"

Megan brushed back a wisp of hair, which had escaped from her ponytail. Glyn could not be sure if it was his imagination, but had he detected a faint blush creep up her neck and flush her cheeks? She actually looked slightly embarrassed. He glanced at her slim, long-legged figure as she sat perched on the high stool. She wore a cream-coloured tee-shirt which clung to her curves, tucked into a pair of dark navy-blue jeans. A blue ribbon tied back her glossy brown hair. She looked very pretty and, all at once, very vulnerable. He had the urge to get up and put his arm around her and ask her what the hell he'd said to unsettle her but managed to restrain himself.

After hesitating for a moment or two she almost whispered, "Well no, actually, I don't. I haven't been on a horse since I was a small girl, and I never really learnt to ride properly."

Damn, why had he just assumed she would be able to ride? Now he'd made her feel uncomfortable, which had not been his intention at all.

"Well, we can soon change that," he replied, in what he hoped sounded like a reassuring tone. "I have a lovely quiet old mare, who would be ideal for you to learn on. What do you say?"

She screwed up her face in the cute, thoughtful way she had sometimes. "Well, um…" she hesitated again. "It's very nice of you but I'm afraid I'm a bit busy tomorrow, perhaps another time. Thanks for the offer though."

Abruptly, she stood and made for the door. Somehow a virtual wall seemed to have come up between them. "Thanks so much for the tea, I must be off now, I was just dropping your dog food off on my way home, and it's getting a bit late."

Glyn nodded, doing his best to hide his disappointment, and followed her to the door. "Not to worry, it was just a thought."

Huw chose that moment to come running in from the stables with Jack at his heels.

"Are you coming tomorrow," he asked gazing up at her, and sounding a little out of breath.

Damn. Perhaps he shouldn't have told his son he intended to ask Megan to go with them for their ride. He seemed to have really taken to her. He hoped Huw was not getting too attached to her. He had a horrible feeling he might have just blown their friendship, although he hadn't realised she could be so sensitive, and really couldn't imagine what he'd said to upset her. After all, he only asked her out for a horse ride with them. Perhaps that Mark person meant more to her than she admitted. He hoped she wouldn't use his stupid invitation as an excuse not to visit anymore.

He hated to think of Huw having to endure another loss. The boy hardly ever asked about her, but Glyn was pretty sure he missed having a mother more than he let on. In a way, he supposed, Huw had begun to look to

Megan to provide the feminine element missing from his life. It must be difficult for him having to grow up without a mother. However hard Glyn tried to fill the role of both parents himself, he knew it wasn't the same.

"No, Megan's busy tomorrow, I'm afraid," he said in a low voice. "I'm sure there are plenty of things we can do together tomorrow, and we can still go for a ride together as usual."

"I'll see you soon, Huw," Megan said, with a wave of her hand.

She walked across to the SUV and drove off without a backward glance, leaving Glyn to wonder how he'd managed to put his foot in it, and if they would actually ever see her at the farm again.

Chapter Nine

Stalemate

Rhiannon drifted near a vase of deep yellow roses Megan had set on the kitchen table earlier in the day. A plate of biscuits materialised beside it.

She settled into a chair in a corner of the kitchen "There, that should make her happy." She paused. "I rather like what she has done to the old place 'tis very comfortable." Without waiting for a reply she went on. "We have to do something about this, you know."

"About what, Rhiannon, cariad? I thought you just said you liked what she has done here."

Rhiannon shook her head and gave him a withering look. "Don't be daft. Not this cottage. Glyn of course, the foolish man who is not able to see what is right in front of him, and that silly girl, Megan."

****

Megan's cheeks still burned, as she drove back to the cottage. How could she tell Glyn the idea of getting on a horse actually terrified her? She bit her lip. Why on earth had she said she was busy the next day when she actually had no plans at all. Why lie? She should have just come straight out and told him the truth. Her hands clenched on the steering wheel, her knuckles turning white, as she recalled the last few minutes. She'd seen the disappointment flash across Glyn's face.

No doubt he'd looked forward to the three of them going out for a ride together. Of course he would have assumed she could ride. She loved animals, she worked for a veterinarian, and she'd told him she lived in the country before her parents moved to London. He probably despised her, thinking her silly and fickle. If she told him the real reason for refusing his invitation now, his estimation of her would go down even further. She sighed. Glyn Phillips' view of her had suddenly become more important than she cared to admit. It had taken a while but she'd finally come to believe not all men were lying, cheating control-freaks like Richard.

When she arrived back at Ty Gwyn the front gate stood slightly ajar. Strange, she would have sworn she'd shut it in the morning when she left for the surgery. Ah well, maybe the postman had been careless and left it open when he delivered the mail. She turned the key in the lock. Sometimes it stuck, and she had difficulty turning it. She really must remember to go to the locksmith in the village and get something done about it. However, this evening it seemed to turn much more easily than usual. She bent to pick up the few items of junk mail and went to put on the soft slippers she always left near the door. She frowned. Drat, they weren't there. She must have been in such a hurry this morning that she'd forgotten to put them ready.

She went into the kitchen and turned on the kettle. She could really use another cup of tea, despite having just had one at Glyn's. Ah, there were her slippers, near her favourite chair, by the little kitchen table.

She slipped them on, grateful for their comfort and surveyed the room while she waited for the kettle to boil. The kitchen looked quite smart now. Cream walls, and blue and white flowered curtains across the windows. The units were light oak and the dark granite worktops gave a modern look while fitting in with the rustic effect of the cupboards and other furnishings. Glyn had said he liked it, and she didn't think he was just being polite. Damn, why couldn't she stop thinking about Glyn? Hadn't she sworn off men—and that should definitely include this one, who, for all she knew, had a wife somewhere. She should have learned from her experience with Richard not to trust a man, however charming he might be on the surface.

She shook her head to banish the memories of Richard. Theirs had not been a particularly passionate affair, but at the time she believed they really were in love. Richard was *something in the city* and seemed to spend his money as fast as he made it. He drove an expensive brand-new car and could not understand why she should be content with an old second-hand model. He'd been quite excited when Megan inherited the cottage and did his best to persuade her to sell it.

"There's a fantastic market in Welsh cottages for holiday homes," he told her. "We could make a killing."

Thinking back after they broke up, she realised he used the word 'we', obviously including himself as benefitting from the profits of the proposed sale. Megan told him she had no intention of selling the cottage as a second home when so many people did not even have a roof over their heads these days. She did not say it out loud, but finally admitted to herself she was tired of city life. The cottage would give her the chance to live the life she secretly yearned for. When she made it clear she had no intention of changing her mind, Richard became more distant and made excuses to be away more and more often. The moment he suddenly announced he thought they should have '*a bit of a break, to work out where our relationship is going*', she knew it was over between them. However, she was not prepared for his engagement to her best friend, Fiona, a few weeks later. On reflection, she should have seen the signs months earlier, but naively she had trusted them both.

She brewed her tea and carried it over to the table. She needed some comfort food and searched around in the cupboard for some chocolate chip cookies. She always kept a stash of them in a tin on the bottom shelf of the cupboard by the window. Strange—it seemed to be empty, apart from a few crumbs. She glanced across at the table. There, by the vase of roses, neatly arranged on a plate with pink flowers around the rim, sat a stack of her favourites. How hadn't she noticed them there before? How odd. She couldn't remember putting them out that morning. She must be more tired than she thought, or perhaps she was losing her mind. Or, she had to admit, as she dunked a cookie in the hot liquid, perhaps her mind had been too much on other things, or to be more honest, other people, like Glyn Phillips.

Her cheeks heated again, recalling her hasty retreat from his farm when he'd invited her to go out riding. What an idiot she was. Why *hadn't* she just explained to him about being petrified at the idea of getting on a horse? She bit her lip. She must have sounded so churlish. Glyn probably thought she was giving him the brush-off. Perhaps he imagined she was seriously thinking of accepting Mark Isaac's offer of a date. If so, what difference would it make to him? Glyn had only suggested a family outing, after all, and just asked her along for company, nothing more. She really valued their friendship, and now she'd probably blown it.

She sighed. As Scarlet O'Hara said, "Tomorrow is another day." So why did it seem as if a dark cloud had suddenly descended over her? And would she ever be able to face Glyn Phillips again?

****

"Just be careful with that pony, Huw. You know, she's given me a few nasty nips on the arm when I've been handling her. I'm not sure I'm altogether happy about you riding her so much."

"She's fine Dad, she is really. She never plays up with me."

"No?" That might be true, but much as he loved horses Glyn was fully aware they could be unpredictable creatures, and this little mare, more than most. He gave the boy a gentle slap on the shoulder. "That doesn't mean she never will. I don't want you to go taking any risks."

He dare not contemplate what he would do if anything happened to the boy. It wasn't easy being a single parent to a growing, strong-willed lad like Huw. Oh, he was a good kid really, but he had a stubborn streak which he must have inherited from his mother, although perhaps he was being a little unfair. If he were being honest, he supposed he could be pretty stubborn himself, sometimes.

He ushered Huw into the kitchen and automatically reminded him to go upstairs and wash his hands. After a quick clean-up in the little downstairs cloakroom, he proceeded to lay the table for their supper of cold meat, and salad. The days were warm, and they could have a barbeque outside the next day. Huw always loved a barbeque. He wondered if he should invite Megan.

He hadn't seen her since he'd invited her to come riding with them.

Glyn sighed. He'd thought they were getting on well, but now she seemed to be keeping her distance. Several times during the week he fetched up her number on his phone, wondering whether to text or call her to ask if she was all right. Each time he put his phone back in his pocket.

What would he say to her? And what would he do if she wanted to end their friendship? Perhaps it was cowardly of him, but he wasn't sure he could handle the rejection. Maybe he should just give her some space for a while. He hoped he hadn't upset her by something he'd said, but he had no idea how to make amends if that were the case. He would just have to wait until dear old Bob needed some more medication and hope she'd offer to drop by with it as usual. Maybe then she would tell him what the hell he'd said to drive her away.

He shrugged his shoulders, trying to banish the sense of something akin to loss. Why should it bother him so much? For heaven's sake, this was the twenty-first century. It wasn't like he'd asked her to move in with him, or even to go out on a date, just an afternoon horse ride.

Women—who could understand them?

Chapter Ten

From Bad to Worse

"We have to try to find some way of getting them together again."

Sion drifted closer to his wife. "Why are you so concerned about those two?"

Rhiannon tossed her head, and her long, dark hair swirled around her shoulders, cascading and tumbling like the froth on a wild Welsh waterfall. "Sion, you know I love you, but you can be rather dim at times. I am a matchmaker, am I not? 'Tis what I do. I just like to see people happy. Glyn is not happy and neither is Megan any more. She has been moping around this last week like a dog without a bone. And if she is not happy, the atmosphere at Ty Gwyn is going to get extremely miserable. It ruins the whole mood of this cottage, it does. I have no wish to exist in a home with a mopey, miserable woman, have you?"

Sion planted a kiss on her cheek. "Well no, I suppose not, seein' as how it will make you all mopey an' miserable, too. What do you suggest?"

Rhiannon tapped her foot with a little sigh of irritation. "Indeed I know not what to do, at the moment. I have to try to think of something though."

****

For the third time that week, Mark Isaac asked

The Matchmaker's Mare

Megan out, and for the third time, she politely refused. Mark seemed nice enough, but he didn't stir her blood and she reminded herself she was not ready to date again. She refused to acknowledge the reason for her reluctance might be Glyn Phillips. They were friends, nothing more, but she could not deny the handsome horse-dealer had made her heart race every time she went near him.

After supper that evening, Megan sat on the bench outside the cottage, her mind in something of a turmoil. Despite her reluctance to form a new relationship, since she'd moved to Ty Gwyn she realised she missed having someone special to go places with, or just to relax and converse with. If Glyn cared anything for their friendship, surely he'd have been in touch by now.

Perhaps he is waiting for you to contact him.

Megan turned sharply, fully expecting to see a woman standing behind her, but could see nothing. Nothing stirred, except a warm breeze blowing through the trees. It wafted the soft scent of lavender toward her, and what sounded like the sound of little tinkling bells which she still hadn't managed to track down.

She must be letting her imagination get the better of her. Or perhaps there really was something in the story Glyn had told her, and the cottage was actually haunted. For the first time since she'd refused his invitation to go riding, she let her lips twitch in a smile. What nonsense.

The thought had merit though. Perhaps they were both waiting for the other to call or text. Well, someone had to make the first move. She decided to pay a casual visit. Nearly a week had passed since that fateful evening. She could always say she wanted to find out how Bob was doing—and ask how Huw was getting on with the chestnut pony.

****

After work Megan found Glyn, as usual, down at the stables. She walked across the yard to the haybarn where he stood filling a haynet, and she hovered in the doorway. "Good evening Glyn."

He turned quickly and a broad smile passed across his face.

"Well, hello, Megan. I'd begun to think you'd forgotten about us."

"I just wondered how Bob is doing now—and how is Huw?"

"That boy of mine spends every spare minute with the pony." He nodded toward the back of the barn and whistled. "Bob's doing so much better now, see for yourself." The corgi bounded up to Glyn, wagging his tail.

Megan bent to pat the old dog's head, and he thumped his tail even harder.

Glyn put the haynet down just outside the door and turned back to Megan. "He's moving much more easily now. The medication is certainly doing a good job." He nodded in the direction of the paddocks. "I think Huw's out in the far field with Seren and Jack. Do you want to hang around until he comes back, I'll call him on his mobile if you like."

"No, don't interrupt him if he's riding. I-I just wanted to…" her voice trailed away. This was harder than she'd thought. "I wanted to explain why I didn't want to go riding last weekend when you asked me."

Glyn raised a quizzical eyebrow. "I have to admit I was a bit anxious about the way you left so suddenly, especially since we haven't seen you since. Did I say something to upset you?"

"No, no. Of course not. I'm sorry, I didn't mean to worry you. It's just—" she bit her lip. "I-I didn't want to admit to you that—that I'm scared."

His face took on an expression of concern, and he stepped closer and laid a hand lightly on her arm. "What…of horses?"

"Not exactly. I'm not really afraid of them, and it's not that I don't like horses, although I've not had a lot to do with them. No, I'm just afraid to get on one. When you asked me to go riding with you and Huw, I was…well, I suppose I was embarrassed to tell you I can't ride."

"There's nothing to be embarrassed about. Not everyone who lives in the countryside can ride a horse—or even wants to. I can teach you if you'd like me to. As I told you, I have a lovely quiet mare who would be ideal for you to start on. She's a real confidence giver."

Megan shifted uneasily from one foot to the other, unable to look him in the eye. "It's not quite so simple. You see—you see I had a bad fall from a horse when I was a youngster, and the thought of getting on one now gives me the jitters." The thought actually made her feel sick, but Glyn was so enthusiastic when it came to horses, she felt ashamed to admit it.

He looked at her, his brows knitting in a frown, his deep brown eyes meeting hers with what looked like surprise rather than the scorn she'd feared.

"Why didn't you tell me you were scared of riding a horse before, when I first asked you?" he asked, his tone gentle.

"I-I was afraid you'd think me feeble and not want to continue our friendship."

The frown deepened, and Megan stepped back a few paces, as he dropped his hand from her arm. "Indeed," he said, his voice now several degrees cooler. "Do you really think I'm such a shallow character I would drop you as a friend just because you're afraid to ride? I didn't realise you thought so little of me."

"No, that's not what I meant. I—" She turned away, feeling the tears spring to her eyes. This was going all wrong. Why hadn't she just told him in the first place and avoided this awkward situation As she'd said, it wasn't even as if she didn't like horses. She did. They were beautiful creatures. She loved all animals, and if it hadn't been for the accident as a child, she'd have welcomed the chance to go riding with Glyn Phillips. "I-I was afraid you wouldn't understand," she stammered. "Obviously I was right. I shouldn't have said anything."

Glyn gave something like a sigh, although since Megan had half turned away from him, she couldn't be completely sure.

"Then perhaps you'd better go out with Mark Isaac next time he asks you, *he* might be a bit more understanding." The words were spoken so softly, she wondered for a moment if he'd actually meant her to hear them. Well, she had, and he couldn't unsay them now.

He turned, picking up the haynet and walked out of the barn without another word. Megan stood looking after him for a long moment, wondering whether to go back to him, to apologise, make this right. Well, why should she? It wasn't her fault if Glyn was so sensitive

The Matchmaker's Mare

he took her reluctance to tell him about her fears so personally. She'd already apologised once, now it was his turn. She waited for several minutes, in the vain hope he would come back and tell her he hadn't meant what he said, but of course, he didn't. She pursed her lips. Perhaps he was right. Mark Isaac had asked her out enough times and perhaps now would be the right time to move on. Admittedly he had nowhere near the same effect on her Glyn did, but there was no denying his attractiveness and charisma—and he wasn't likely to ask her to get on the back of a horse any time soon, either. She stomped back to the SUV and slammed the door.

Goodbye Glyn Phillips, you can get your own prescriptions in future. I'm finished with you, You're not my only friend, and there are plenty of other fish in the sea!

****

Glyn went into the adjoining feed room and scooped several measures of feed into a bucket, angry at himself. Why on Earth had he said that? He could only hope she hadn't heard the words he'd mumbled—and why hadn't he been a bit more sympathetic and understanding? Megan was sweet and sensitive. He should have accepted the fact she'd feel embarrassed about telling him of her fear of riding instead of letting his pride get the better of him.

He took the net he'd just filled with fresh, aromatic hay and carried it and the feed bucket to the end loosebox. He tipped the feed into the manger and tied the haynet on a ring high enough for the mare to reach easily, without getting a foot caught in it.

He stroked the glossy black neck of the horse and

ran a hand over her flank. "Any day now Ebony, old girl," he murmured. "You kept this one a secret, didn't you. I really didn't think you were going to give us a foal this year." With a final gentle pat, he left the mare to enjoy her meal.

He cursed under his breath and hastened his stride. He'd been so afraid he'd say something else without thinking and really put his foot in it, he'd just left Megan standing by the barn. Better apologise to her before she decided to leave.

He heard the car door slam but by the time he'd crossed the yard, Megan's vehicle was gone. Damn! Had she heard the words he'd meant to say under his breath, after all? He really hadn't meant to upset her. The fact she hadn't felt she could confide her fear of riding to him when he first asked her if she wanted to ride, had bothered and unsettled him. It hurt, and he'd spoken just now without thinking Perhaps he'd been oversensitive, but he believed they were friends. In fact, in the past few weeks, he had the feeling they were becoming close, perhaps on the verge of being something more than friends in the future. Now he'd probably blown it for good and wrecked any chance he might have had of ever taking their relationship further.

He'd been complacent, comfortable with their easy friendship. For a moment, he'd been so wounded by her words he said the first thing that came to mind, without thinking of the effect his muttered words might have on her. He voiced the thing he'd feared—the notion she might take up with her new admirer. And now he'd encouraged her into the arms of that very man.

Chapter Eleven

The Date

"So that didn't work out too well, did it now?"

"Well, I tried. 'Tis not my fault those two are so sensitive and insist on misunderstanding each other, like a couple of children." Rhiannon sighed and blew gently on a pot of flowers which had begun to fade. Immediately they revived and her expression changed to one of satisfaction for a moment. *"At least I can do something to raise Megan's spirits a little."*

She waved a hand and a pair of Megan's favourite earrings slid out from between the pages of a novel in the bookcase and floated into the bedroom, where Rhiannon directed them into the little jewellery box on Megan's dressing table.

She wagged an accusing finger at Sion. *"And she can do without you playing silly tricks on her and hiding things, too. 'Tis not amusing. One of these days you'll become careless, and she will see you, and you will scare the poor girl out of her wits."*

Sion rose from the arm of Megan's comfortable easy chair and planted a kiss on her cheek, but Rhiannon would not be so easily appeased.

"And I have not forgiven you yet for taking my pony and leaving her with Glyn Phillips. Why did you have to go and do such a stupid thing anyway?"

Sion grinned sheepishly. "Still on about that, love? Well, you see, I thought it would give you something to moan at me about..."

He ducked as a cushion rose from the comfortable sofa and sailed across the room, narrowly missing his head.

"You can be really foolish sometimes, Sion Sienco. It was a really daft thing to do."

"No need to call me foolish, cariad. 'Twas only a joke. I knew it would not take you long to track her down."

"But now the boy has gone and bonded with her. Sion, you drive me insane sometimes, you do. She is my pony, but now he rides her and thinks of her as his own..."

"Well, how was I to know he had such empathy with horses and would be able to tame her? Anyway, we've already agreed Seren helped bring Megan and Glyn together."

Rhiannon shook her head, refusing to let him off the hook. "You even gave her a solid form. Did it never occur to you to think maybe they might want to keep her? And what if Glyn had just sold her? Now that would have led me a merry dance, would it not!"

"Might have given me a bit of peace..."

"What was that?" Rhiannon demanded.

"Nothin', cariad, nothin'."

Another cushion sailed through the air and to any casual observer it would have looked like it had taken flight all by itself. A sound, like a young woman giggling, carried on the wind.

****

A week passed, and Megan could not put her

argument with Glyn out of her mind, however hard she tried. She kept churning it over and over in her head. How had it started anyway? She couldn't even remember. One minute Glyn had been looking at her with a gentle, even sympathetic expression in his eyes, the next he'd been accusing her—of what? Of thinking him shallow? That's what it sounded like, and the last thing she'd intended.

Several more days passed, and she heard nothing from Glyn. He had enough dog food, and medication for Bob to last for a few more weeks. Barring a problem with one of the horses or the dogs, he had no need to contact the surgery. He did not call or text her personally, and she felt too embarrassed to call him. The awkwardness of their last meeting preyed on her mind, and she found it hard to think of anything else.

After two more weeks and still no word from Glyn. Megan decided to stop hoping for a rekindling of their friendship. She missed stopping by on her way back to the cottage. She'd enjoyed chatting with him and his son, but the more time went on, the harder it became to contemplate facing him and explaining why she stupidly left in such a hurry.

She'd been asked to work late for the last fortnight, as Mair had been on annual leave.

To be fair, Megan had volunteered. In the unlikely event Glyn came into the surgery, and asked why she'd stopped calling, she could say truthfully it was late by the time she finished work. Too bad she even needed an excuse though. She hated the situation between them and longed for things to get back to the way they had been.

On the Friday evening, as she left the surgery,

Mark stood outside waiting for her.

"Good evening, Gorgeous. You know I'm not going to give up until you agree to have dinner with me."

Despite her reservations, Megan could not help admiring his persistence. She allowed herself a smile. After all most women would be flattered by his attentions, and it had been a long time since she'd had anything resembling a date.

She nodded. "All right, you win. Tomorrow night, then?" She almost laughed out loud at the look of surprise on his face.

"Fantastic. I'll pick you up at your place at about seven thirty, okay?"

"Yes, fine. Thanks, I'll see you then."

She gave him a wave and unlocked her car, hoping she was doing the right thing. While not particularly keen to start dating again, it had been a while since she'd been out for an evening, and it might make a pleasant change. She had nothing better to do, after all. Arriving back at the cottage, she sank onto a chair in the kitchen, all at once assailed by doubts. After a minute or two, she pulled out her mobile phone from her pocket and brought up Bethan's number. After a few rings, she heard the familiar voice at the other end.

"Hello Megan, everything all right, is it?"

"Oh hi, Bethan. I just wanted to say…that is, I've agreed to have dinner with Mark tomorrow night."

"Well there's a surprise. Wore you down, did he now?"

"Yes—well sort of. The thing is, I'm—I'm not sure if it's right for me to go out with him, in case he gets the wrong idea. You see…" she hesitated, searching for the right words. "He's very nice, and good looking and everything, but, well I don't quite know how I feel about him. I don't think I want to get serious at the moment, and I don't want to seem to be leading him on. I'm not that sort of person Bethan—"

She heard something like a chuckle at the other end. "Listen here Megan, my girl, Mark fancies you like mad. He's always been able to get any woman he wanted. It will do him good if you make it clear you're not prepared to be one of his conquests. Go ahead and enjoy yourself. If you don't want another date, just tell him. He'll get over it. Just make sure you're not the one who gets hurt."

Megan thanked her and put the phone back in her pocket, still not entirely convinced she'd made the right decision in agreeing to go out with Mark. Then she tossed her hair back and walked over to the fridge to find something for her evening meal. Bethan seemed sure there was no problem. After all, it was only a dinner date, and she'd offer to go Dutch, so she wouldn't feel she owed him anything. Of course, there was always the chance they would hit it off, and it would lead to something meaningful. Something to make her forget all about Glyn Phillips.

****

On Saturday morning Megan ambled through the woodland behind the cottage, enjoying the smell of the damp grass after an early morning shower of rain.

Visiting the Phillips farm most weekends, and walking with Huw and the young dog his father was helping him train had become a habit. Now she felt at a bit of a loss. Once she'd done the housework and pottered around the garden, there was not a great deal to do apart from walking and trying to think of something else besides Glyn Phillips. For the first time since she'd come to live in Ty Gwyn, she did not even have the heart to paint.

Again, she wished she had a dog, but knew it wouldn't be fair to leave a dog by itself for hours, while she was at work. Because they were so busy at the surgery her part-time hours had now stretched into nearly a full day. Sometimes the girls in the office would bring their own dogs in for the day, but she probably wouldn't be allowed to do it on a daily basis.

She found her mind drifting to Hafod Farm again. Glyn was probably out riding with his son now. If only she hadn't had that nasty fall when she was a youngster, she might have been sharing this time with them both, instead of walking alone in the woods. Yet again she asked herself why on Earth hadn't she just been straight with him and told him she was scared to ride when he first asked her. He might have thought her a bit feeble, but at least they would still be friends. Ah well, at least she had dinner with Mark to look forward to.

Later, after showering and preparing for her date, Megan spent some time deciding what to wear. Should she go casual, or would it be better to dress up a bit? She had no idea where Mark intended to take her for their meal, he had indicated he would book somewhere *quiet*, but that could mean anything. In the end, she decided on a pair of black velvet slacks and a silky gold-coloured blouse. *Casual smart*, so hopefully it would not look too out of place in a smart restaurant, but equally would not be over the top in a more downmarket establishment. Should she wear her hair up or down? In the end, she settled for tying it back at the nape of her neck, secured with a large, pretty hair slide.

Mark picked her up in his smart sports car at seven-thirty prompt.

"You look stunning," he said, opening the passenger side door for her, before walking around to the driver's seat.

He drove to a small, secluded restaurant in the next village. The waiter showed them to a table in the corner by a large window overlooking a stream meandering through an expanse of grassland.

Mark held her chair for her and after she took her seat, ordered a bottle of wine while they perused the menu. Megan had not been out for a meal for a while, and she began to enjoy the experience. Perhaps this evening would not be so bad after all. Following the starter, she chose Chicken Cordon Bleu while Mark ordered steak au poivre for himself.

They ate most of the meal in silence, with the occasional polite attempt at conversation. It didn't take long for her to realise she and Mark had little in common. Unlike his sister, he did not seem particularly fond of animals. He confessed to not reading very much and the films he enjoyed watching were mainly war films, while Megan preferred rom-coms or mysteries.

For dessert, she chose raspberry cheesecake with Devon cream and Mark ordered the same.

"What sort of hobbies do you like?" she asked, in between mouthfuls of cheesecake, in an attempt to try and find something in common they could talk about.

"I play rugby whenever I can," he said, with more enthusiasm than he had shown all evening. "Can't get enough of it. How about you?"

"I'm afraid I'm not much into sports," she

confessed. "I like walking, but my main interest is painting." He nodded, but he did not ask for more details, and Megan did not offer them. The evening dragged on and after they finished the meal, he asked if she would like a coffee, but she politely refused. She preferred tea anyway and couldn't face the thought of another fifteen or so minutes trying to make pointless conversation. She insisted on paying for her half of the meal, although Mark politely made a show of refusing. However, to her relief, he did not make too much of an effort to dissuade her from paying her share.

The moon had risen when they left the restaurant, shafts of moonlight reflecting on the waters of the stream mingled with the lights from the restaurant. Megan took a deep breath of the cool evening air, smiling in appreciation of the beauty before her. Mark held the door open for her and she slid into the passenger seat. She relaxed into the seat and closed her eyes. Perhaps it hadn't been such a bad night, even if it hadn't turned out to be the sparkling occasion she might have wished for.

They pulled up outside the cottage, and Mark went round to open the door for her. At least she couldn't fault his impeccable manners. He walked with her to the door. Should she ask him in for a tea or coffee? She decided against it. He probably expected her to invite him in, but it might give him the wrong impression and, as she'd told Bethan, she had no intention of leading him on. She sighed inwardly. The evening had not been unpleasant, but she did not have any wish to take it further.

"Thank you for a lovely evening," she said. "It was a really good meal, I've never been to that restaurant before."

"I'm glad you enjoyed it. We must do it again."

"Er, yes…" Megan mumbled, searching around in her bag for her key.

Without warning, he put a hand on her bottom, pulled her against him and into his arms, and attempted to kiss her.

She pulled back and turned her head quickly so as to present her cheek, but he placed a firm hand on her chin and tried to force his lips onto hers.

"No—no, don't please," she gasped. "Just stop." He gripped her harder and again tried to kiss her.

Megan pushed her hand into his chest and wrenched herself out of his grasp, barely resisting the urge to slap his face. "I'm sorry, I'm just not ready for this—" she said sharply.

He glared at her in the moonlight and for a moment she feared he would try to grab hold of her again, but to her relief, he scowled and stepped back. "Why did you lead me on if you had no intention of making it worth my while," he almost spat out. He turned without another word and went back to the car, got in and slammed the door, driving off at speed back up the lane.

She let out a long breath. He might not have set her heart on fire, but until now he had been courteous and respectful. She'd not expected this—or was she being too sensitive again? Perhaps all he wanted was a goodnight kiss, and it had been churlish of her to refuse. However, in her heart, she knew he'd probably have wanted more than just a chaste kiss, however polite and gallant he might have seemed earlier. What was the matter with her? When it came to men, it seemed she had no clue. Why did she even bother to try?

She unlocked the cottage door and seated herself at the table in the kitchen, kicking off her shoes and resting her head in her hands.

Why had she ever agreed to go out on that stupid date in the first place? To spite Glyn Phillips? If she was honest with herself there was more than a grain of truth in the idea, but then, he'd been the one to suggest it in the first place. How could either of them know someone like Mark, who appeared so solid and dependable on the surface, would turn into someone who thought it was all right to grab a woman and try to kiss her on their first date.

Come on, girl, she told herself with a resigned shrug, *we're not living in the dark ages—plenty of women will kiss a man on their first date—and a lot more.*

She sighed. Well, it might be the case for plenty of women, but she was not one of them. She should have learnt her lesson with Richard. Men always let you down, she should forget them and concentrate on animals—at least you knew where you stood with a dog or a cat—or even a horse, for that matter.

****

The following Monday

When Megan finished her morning shift at the surgery, she popped her head into the side office where she knew Bethan would be having lunch. For once, she hadn't been asked to work any extra hours, so she would try to get back to painting when she returned to the cottage. What was the point in wasting her life moping? Time to get back to doing what she loved.

To her relief, Bethan was the only one in the room. She knew Bethan and her brother were close. He had probably told her about their disastrous date.

"Hi Megan," Bethan said, looking up from her sandwich. "Are you having lunch here today?"

"No, I'm just off for the day, but I wondered…have you seen your brother?"

"Mark? Yes, I saw him this morning before I came in."

"I suppose he told you what happened Saturday night?"

"Well, of course you told me you'd arranged to have dinner with him, and I asked about it. He didn't say much, although I gather you made quite an impression on him, but I got the feeling you probably wouldn't be having a second date."

Megan heaved a sigh of relief. So he hadn't made her out to be a tease who led men on to expect more than she was prepared to give. That, at least, was something to be thankful for.

Bethan laid a friendly hand on her arm. "I don't want to poke my nose in where it's not wanted like, but I did warn you Mark is a bit of a 'lady-killer'. You don't have to go into details if you don't want to, but I know how he works. He'll wine and dine a woman until she falls under his spell, then it's a one night stand and he drops her like a hot potato. It doesn't mean there's anything wrong with you, it's just the way he operates."

Megan gave her a wan smile. "Actually, he didn't drop me, I dropped him, in a manner of speaking. He made a pass at me, and I just wasn't ready for it."

At least Bethan seemed to know all about her brother's cavalier attitude when it came to women. She had been afraid she would take his side, and really didn't want to lose her as a friend.

"Thanks for understanding," she said simply.

"Mark's going to come a cropper, one day," Bethan said. "I'm just sorry he tried it on with you. I did try to warn you not to take his advances too seriously."

"Don't worry," Megan told her. "I'm a big girl now, and I wasn't harbouring any illusions."

"I must admit I was quite surprised when you told me you'd agreed to go out with him. You've turned him down so many times, I thought he'd have got the message by now." She paused, with a little grin. "I always thought you and Glyn Phillips might get together."

Megan felt herself blush to the roots of her hair.

"Oh my gosh," Bethan cried, "you *do* have the *hots* for him, don't you?"

"He's one of the nicest, most charming men I've ever met," Megan said, trying not to sound defensive. "But there's nothing going on between us, we're just friends." She paused for a moment. "Anyway, we haven't seen each other for a while now."

"That's a shame," Bethan said. "I reckon the two of you would have made a perfect couple."

"Well, it's not likely to happen," Megan told her with a shrug. "Besides, we still don't know if he has a wife or not." She hoped she'd managed to keep her expression indifferent. She could only be thankful no one knew about the sketch of Glyn Phillips still hidden in a locked drawer in her desk at home.

When she returned to Ty Gwyn a long, narrow package sat on the doorstep. Her heart leapt. Perhaps it was a peace offering from Glyn. She managed to open the door, with the box underneath her arm, without dropping the keys. She went into the kitchen and opened the box with trembling fingers. Inside was a large bouquet of mixed pale yellow and red roses.

****

For about the fifth time in a week, Glyn checked Bob's prescription. A week's supply still left, and several more weeks of the food. He sighed. No real reason to pop into the vets then.

Three weeks had passed since their stupid quarrel, and of course he had only himself to blame. How could he have been so insensitive? He missed Megan's company, their chats, her laugh, the way she tossed her hair back sometimes, reminding him of a frisky pony

He'd hardly even glanced at another woman since Clarissa left, until he met Megan, and then he only thought of her as a friend—didn't he? He'd kept himself to himself and had certainly not gone out of his way to meet anyone else. He and Huw managed fine by themselves and did not need anyone else. So why did he miss Megan so much now? He patted Bob's head when the dog came and rubbed himself against his leg. "Yes, boy, you miss her too, don't you?"

He wondered if he should text her. Just a casual message asking how she was, and saying Huw wanted to know when they would see her again, which was true. Then he reminded himself she was probably having a much better time with Mark what's-his-name than she ever could with him. No point in texting her. He'd had enough of rejection.

He'd been perfectly happy before Megan Johnson walked into his life, and he could darned well be just as happy without her.

Chapter Twelve

An Olive Branch

Rhiannon sat slumped on the window seat overlooking the garden "I cannot help it, Sion. I have to do something. Megan does not look like she wants to make the first move, does she? Sion, leave her shoes where they are," she said sharply. "Stop your foolishness. Megan could come back from work at any moment."

"Perhaps you should leave well alone, cariad, have you not thought she may be a lost cause."

"Lost cause? Lost cause indeed. Listen Sion Sienco, there is no way I will give up on this one."

"Seems to me Glyn Phillips might be easier to persuade then."

Rhiannon considered for a moment. "I do not know. Perhaps I should think about going to Hafod Farm and having a word in Glyn's ear. I cannot be sure if it would work though. Although this cottage is Megan's home now, 'tis also the only home I've ever known as well. You could say 'tis my domain."

"And mine too," Sion reminded her before going on quickly, "so you think your connection with this cottage is the reason you can get into Megan's thoughts? Like the other day when you managed to make her think it was a good idea to go to Hafod Farm

and try to explain to Glyn—"

Rhiannon screwed up her face. "I thank you for reminding me about that. It did not work out the way I had hoped at all. My intention was never for her to go out with that Mark fellow."

"So, what are you goin' to do?"

"I suppose I will just have to see if I can get through to Megan again. I will not give up on those two."

****

Megan placed the bouquet on the table, beside the florist's box, and removed the handwritten card.

"Dear Megan," it read. *"I'm so sorry about Saturday night. I shouldn't have taken so much for granted or tried to rush things. I'm not sure what got into me. I haven't been able to stop thinking about you. Can we try again? Please text or phone me on this number."*

The card was signed: *"Mark".*

Megan's first reaction was one of disappointment the flowers weren't from Glyn, then of surprise that Mark would actually apologise.

She put aside the thought she should send them back. If Mark was sincere in his apology then she could at least accept it gracefully. She would have written a proper note if she knew his address, but instead had to resort to a polite text. She thanked him for the roses, saying while she bore no ill feelings, she didn't feel she wanted to pursue a relationship at the moment, and wishing him well. She hit 'send', wondering if she'd done the right thing. Perhaps she should have given him another chance? No, it wouldn't work. Even if he'd changed from the *lady killer* his sister said he was, she knew she could never really feel anything for him. They just didn't have anything in common. Besides, she had to admit only one man had the power to make her blood heat whenever he was near her. A man who invaded her thoughts far too much. She'd believed she would never let another man charm his way into her heart again, but that was before she met Glyn Phillips.

Megan spent the early part of the afternoon by the river, trying to paint but found she still couldn't concentrate and packed her painting gear away. Returning to the cottage she spent a few hours in the garden picking several baskets of soft fruit. The season had been good, and her fruit bushes were loaded. Later that evening she prepared the fresh raspberries, strawberries, and blackcurrants for the freezer, together with some sweet cherries from the trees in the little orchard behind the cottage. They would be good to make fruit pies with, in the winter, but some she would use now. She had enough fruit laid aside to make two or three good-sized crumbles. She could have one after supper tonight and freeze the other two.

Or you could always take one over to Glyn as a kind of olive branch. Come on Megan, you know you are miserable, not seeing him.

Where did *that* thought come from? For a moment, Megan almost imagined someone whispered the words in her ear. She looked around, but of course saw no one there. How could there be? She had few visitors and always kept the front door locked in the evening, just in case. Intruders or burglars in this area were unlikely, but she'd seen a report online recently about rural crime becoming more prevalent, and there was no point in taking unnecessary risks. If anyone tried to enter the house, she would have heard them.

This wasn't the first time she'd heard voices, or to be more accurate *a* voice. Was the cottage really haunted? She shrugged an impatient shoulder. What nonsense. Obviously, her overactive imagination was playing tricks, and her subconscious now had her talking to herself. There were no such things as ghosts, and anyway, wasn't the air in a room haunted by a ghost supposed to feel several degrees colder than normal? The cottage always felt warm, despite, or perhaps because of, the stone walls, especially on a lovely summer's day like today.

She gave herself a mental shake and took the flour and sugar from the cupboard.

It is an idea though. Someone has to make the first move. You could drop the fruit crumble in at the farm tomorrow, after work, and see how the land lies.

There she was, talking to herself again. Why couldn't she get Glyn out of her mind? His last words to her still stung, but she supposed she had been a bit short with him as well. She'd practically accused him of not being capable of understanding about her being scared of riding a horse. She bit her lip. She missed her visits to the farm more than she cared to admit—as well as Glyn's company.

She picked up a slab of butter she'd placed on the side to soften and cut it up to put in the mixing bowl with the flour and sugar. It took only a few minutes to turn the flour, sugar, and butter into fine crumbs for the crumble, with a good pinch of cinnamon to bring out the flavour. She scooped the prepared fruit into three oven and freezer-proof pie dishes and distributed the crumble evenly into each of them, then sprinkled a little more brown cane sugar on top. She could bake two and still have one for the freezer, ready to bake another day.

Soon the aroma of fruit and cinnamon filled the kitchen. By the time they were cooked, she knew she had to give in to the insistent thoughts in her head.

She hummed softly to herself, her spirits lifting, thinking how she would surprise Glyn the next day.

****

Glyn heard a vehicle pull up in the yard as he placed a warm mash in the manger and gave the mare an affectionate rub on the neck. He turned round to look over the half door to see who it was, and nearly dropped the empty feed bucket.

Lifting the catch on the stable door, he hoped he wasn't hallucinating as Megan stepped from the SUV. He set the feed bucket on the ground, his heart skipping a beat, and closed the half door behind him. He walked over to her, trying not to show his surprise and delight at seeing her again.

"Hello," he said, keeping his voice normal with an effort. "It's been such a long time, I wasn't sure we'd be seeing you again."

"I've had to work late a lot recently, one of the girls has been on leave." She dropped her gaze, and he wondered if that was an excuse. There were so many times when he'd wanted to send her a text, to find out if she was all right, or ring her mobile, just to hear her voice. His courage had failed him on each occasion. He had been afraid she'd ignore his calls, and the silence was better than a rebuff.

She gave a hint of a smile, raising her head, but not quite looking at him, and brought a tinfoil package from behind her back.

"I brought you a fresh fruit crumble," she went on a little hesitantly. "Peace offering. It just needs heating up for a few minutes in the microwave, or a bit longer in the oven." She hesitated again for a moment, but before he could speak, she went on. "I wanted to apologise. Honestly, I didn't mean to offend you, it wasn't that I didn't trust you—I mean—" The words came out in something of a rush, and he couldn't help smiling, relief flooding over him. She had come to apologise—and all this time he'd been wondering how to make amends for the way he'd spoken to her the last time she'd visited, and if she'd ever forgive him.

"Woah," he held up his hand. "I'm the one who should be apologising. I should have been more understanding. It's not your fault you had a bad experience with horses, and I should never have said what I did. You just took me by surprise a bit, that's all." He took the crumble from her and offered what he hoped was a suitably apologetic smile. "Thank you, that's kind of you."

"Then we're still friends?"

"Yes, of course." Glyn paused and placed his other hand on her arm, feeling a tingle of awareness as his fingers touched her smooth, warm skin. "I value your friendship more than you know. I'd hate to think I'd lost it."

"So would I. Then let's just put that silly misunderstanding behind us, shall we?"

He stifled the urge to pull her into his arms and tell her how he really felt. Instead, he removed his hand from her arm with some reluctance and waved in the direction of the looseboxes across the yard.

"Come with me, there's something you might like

to see." He guided her to the corner loosebox and told her to peek over the door.

"Oh, isn't it adorable," she breathed, her gaze lingering on the black mare standing over a tiny foal, the image of its mother."

"A pretty pair, aren't they?" Glyn said, smiling with a certain amount of pride. "The filly's a late foal. All the others were born in the spring. This one arrived early this morning. Until a few months ago I didn't even think the mare *was* in foal."

"She's gorgeous." Together they watched the long-legged foal suckle from its mother, and he could tell the foal enchanted her. Megan's love of animals shone from her face, despite the nervousness she'd confessed to, where horses were concerned. It seemed, from what she said though, being on board a horse rather than the horses themselves, was what scared her.

"Her name's *Deryn Du,*" he told her. "It means 'Blackbird.' Look, why don't you stop for a while and have a meal with us?" he went on, "It's only a bit of ham salad, but you're welcome to share with us—there's plenty for three, and your crumble will finish it off nicely."

"I—well, thanks, if you're sure."

"Of course, we'll be glad of your company, and we do owe you a meal."

She smiled her shy little smile which lit up her face and he found so enchanting. "If you insist. Thank you."

They walked up to the house together, and Glyn wondered if she had any idea of the effect she had on him. Huw was already there before them. He jumped up and down when he saw her, not attempting to hide his pleasure at seeing her again.

"Hello Megan, I saw your car in the yard. I'm so glad you've come here again."

"It's lovely to see you, too," she said, smiling. I've been a bit busy, lately. Your dad's been showing me the new foal."

Huw grabbed hold of her sleeve and led her into the living room, chatting all the while. Clearly Glyn was not the only one who'd missed Megan's visits.

Glyn laid out the meal, and while they ate, they engaged in casual chit chat. Glyn wondered how to broach the subject which had been playing on his mind ever since their disagreement.

"That was delicious," he said, as he polished off the last of Megan's fruit crumble, served with a good dollop of ice cream.

"I'm glad you enjoyed it, it's such a simple recipe, but a good way to use up the summer berries."

They left the table and sat by the window and chatted for a while about the new foal, and Huw's schoolwork.

Eventually, Glyn glanced at his watch. The time had flown, and he liked Huw to be in bed by 9 p.m. on school nights.

"It's gone eight o'clock and you haven't finished your homework yet," he reminded him. "You'd better go up now and do it before bedtime, I'll come up and see you a bit later."

"Aw Dad, do I have to?"

"Yes, you do. It's Friday tomorrow, and you'll have all weekend to ride Seren, and go to bed a bit later."

With a few grumbles, Huw fetched his schoolbag, said goodnight to Megan and obediently went on up to his room.

"He's a good kid really," Glyn told Megan. "I just have to play the 'heavy-handed father' on occasion."

"I think you're doing a great job. It can't be easy raising a young boy all by yourself."

"No," he said, heavily. "Since my wife left me, I've had to learn to be both father and mother to Huw. As you say, it hasn't been easy, but we manage." He didn't want to dwell on the subject. Clarissa was the last thing he wanted to be talking to Megan about.

A look he couldn't quite interpret passed across her face.

"Is that a photograph of your parents?" she asked nodding toward the photograph of a middle-aged couple on the mantle, as if realising he was reluctant to go into more details.

He nodded. "Yes, it is. They live in Anglesey now, but they visit occasionally." He frowned. This was another subject difficult to talk about. When Glyn announced his intention to marry Clarissa, they'd made no secret of their disapproval, and a coolness developed between them when he refused to listen to their advice. He'd been young and foolish and paid the price. He deeply regretted their falling out. Without their help, both financially and practically, he would not have been able to buy the farm in South Wales and start his pony training and breeding enterprise. They made up after Clarissa left him, and his parents were incredibly fond of their grandson, although he knew he hadn't taken him to see them as often as he should.

"How are things at the vets?" he asked, needing to change the subject.

"Busy, as always," she said with a smile. "The

The Matchmaker's Mare

usual cat and dog ailments mainly. Someone came in with an injured hedgehog the other day, and we had to direct them to the wildlife sanctuary."

Glyn nodded, "It's handy having the sanctuary just a couple of miles away. I've had occasion to take them injured wild animals myself, once or twice." He paused. He could not help it, he had to know. "Changing the subject, how did the date with Mark go?" He kept his voice casual and hoped he didn't sound too intrusive.

"How did you know about that?" she asked, flushing a little.

He smiled as nonchalantly as he could. "This is a small community. Word gets around." He hesitated. "I'm sorry. I didn't mean to intrude. Forget I said anything, it's none of my business" He groaned inwardly. They'd just made up. He hoped he hadn't upset her again by putting his big foot in where it wasn't wanted. To his relief, she smiled back.

"I suppose I should have realised there'd be a *bush telegraph*. It was okay," she went on. "I had a good time, but—" she hesitated, and Glyn hoped she would say they wouldn't be having a follow-up date.

"We didn't have an awful lot in common, and to be honest, I'm not sure I'm ready for another relationship yet, my last one ended badly."

Glyn breathed a private sigh of relief, but at the same time warning bells rang. She didn't want another relationship. Well, in any case, he was not in a position to offer her one. Not yet. He had no intention of prying into her past, but he couldn't help hoping he could somehow help her get over whatever bad experience she'd had and to help her to see not all men were the same.

"Would you like another cup of tea?" he asked, feeling like an awkward schoolboy, not sure what to say next, "or would you prefer something stronger?" He needed a drink of something a little stronger himself. He was not a great drinker, but he kept a few bottles in the cabinet for the rare occasions when they'd had visitors or to seal a deal with a client.

"I'd better not have anything alcoholic," she said. "I know it's only a short drive home, but I don't want to take any risks."

"Of course not, I wasn't thinking. How about some of my home-made non-alcoholic elderflower cordial, then?"

"That sounds lovely."

He poured her a glass of the cordial, and a brandy for himself, then settled back in one of the cosy chairs by the fireplace, opposite her. They sat in easy silence while he drank the brandy and she sipped her cordial.

Go on, ask her, you know you want to.

Glyn could have sworn he heard a voice in his head. For Heaven's sake, he'd only had one brandy! Still it seemed to have given him the courage he needed. He paused for a moment, choosing his words carefully. "I don't know how you'd feel about this, but I just wonder, would you like me to teach you to ride? I know you said you were nervous about riding, but sometimes the best way to get over a fear is just to face it. I'll make sure you don't come to any harm, I promise."

She shifted a little uneasily in her chair. "It's very kind of you, but I'm sure you have plenty of things you have to do without bothering about me being scared to ride."

Glyn leaned closer to her, just a little. "Look, I'm sorry if the idea of riding still worries you. If you'd rather not, let's just forget I said anything. The last thing I want to do is force you into doing something you're not happy with, and I certainly don't want any more misunderstandings between us."

She hesitated and Glyn sighed inwardly. Had he stupidly repeated his earlier mistake and blown it for good this time?

Chapter Thirteen

The Riding Lesson

Go on, Megan. He is trying his best so he is. He will not allow anything to happen to you, you can be sure of that. 'Tis not easy for me leaving Ty Gwyn you know, that old house has a sort of hold on me it does. I cannot be sure if you can hear me here at the farm—but I had to try to do something about you two, and I managed to connect with Glyn for a moment. For goodness sake say yes, or I will knock your two silly heads together I will.

****

Megan took a deep breath. This phobia, begun in childhood, had gone on far too long. The gentle, quietly spoken man sitting opposite her had just given her the chance to get over her childhood fears. Surely it would be beyond stupid to refuse. Something seemed to tell her he would make sure she came to no harm, and it would certainly be a good excuse to spend some more time together.

"All right," she said quickly before she had chance to change her mind. "Thank you. Let's do it."

Glyn's answering smile was as infectious as it was reassuring, and she couldn't help smiling back.

"How about after lunch on Saturday," he suggested. "I'm so glad you changed your mind. I

The Matchmaker's Mare

promise you won't regret it."

****

All the way home, Megan couldn't help wondering if her nerve would hold out and if she really could get over her fear of riding. Would she make some excuse to call it off? She also mulled over the information Glyn let drop. His wife wasn't dead. She'd left him and was presumably very much alive. On the other hand, he'd had to bring his son up by himself, and although he hadn't said they were divorced, it didn't seem like he expected her to come back anytime soon.

She sighed. Of course, that didn't necessarily mean he was free to pursue another relationship either, which was probably just as well. She wasn't really interested in one herself, despite the feelings for Glyn she tried so hard to suppress. Once bitten, twice shy, as the saying went. Nevertheless, that did not mean she could not be glad they were still friends.

****

When Saturday morning arrived. Megan woke, with a feeling of trepidation she tried to dismiss. She showered, slipped into a short-sleeved shirt and donned a pair of denim jeans. They would do to start with. If by some miracle she decided she wanted more than just one lesson, she might invest in some proper riding clothes.

After a light breakfast she went for a walk to quell her nerves. After lunch, she grabbed her new riding helmet from the small table in the hall and took a deep breath. Glyn had told her he would like her to wear a riding hat, just in case, although he emphasised, she was very unlikely to fall off. She hoped he was right. At least by making the purchase, she was also making a commitment, in case she'd felt like backing down at the last minute.

"You look like you're ready for business," Glyn said, as she stepped out of her SUV, riding hat in hand. "I've told Huw there are some looseboxes in need of mucking out before he goes to ride Seren." He smiled encouragingly. "I didn't think you'd want an audience for your first riding lesson with me!"

Megan smiled back, grateful for his consideration. Huw might only be a boy, and she had a great relationship with him, but she felt nervous enough without having the added distraction of an onlooker.

"Come and meet Flicka." Glyn led her across to the row of neat looseboxes and stopped at the third one along. A dark bay mare, with a small white half-moon shaped flash in the middle of her face, looked over the half-door and whickered softly. Glyn fished a carrot out of his pocket and offered it to the horse who crunched happily. "Here, you give her one," he suggested, handing her another one from his seemingly bottomless pocket. "It will help her to get to know you and build up a relationship."

Megan held the carrot out in the palm of her hand, and Flicka took the treat gently, without hesitation, making short work of it. The horse's lips were soft, and Megan couldn't help smiling as the whiskers under Flicka's chin tickled her palm.

Glyn took a halter from a hook on the wall by the half door. "You said you were thrown by a horse when you were young. How old were you, and had you done much riding?"

"Oh, I think I was a couple of years older than Huw," Megan said, trying to recall memories she'd

The Matchmaker's Mare

pushed to the back of her mind for so long. "We were on holiday one summer. We stayed at a small hotel in the Lake District, and there were some riding stables nearby. My mother thought it would be fun to have a few riding lessons. The first day was fine. We were taught the basics and just walked around the schooling paddock for an hour. The second day we decided to be more adventurous and go out for a ride along the lanes, but a dog suddenly appeared from nowhere and scared my pony. It threw me and I fell awkwardly, breaking my wrist. I haven't been on a horse since."

"That's a real shame," Glyn said, his voice sympathetic. "Riding on horseback is such a great way to see the countryside, and there's nothing quite like the relationship a rider can build with a horse." He paused for a moment. "So will it be okay with you if I treat you like a raw beginner?"

"Please do," she told him. "To be honest, I can't really remember much about my first lesson. I just hope I won't try your patience too much." She raised a tentative hand and stroked the mare's nose as she spoke, and Flicka blew softly through her nostrils, making her laugh.

"She seems to like you," Glyn said approvingly. "You're not really scared of horses, are you?"

"No, I'm not scared of them, not really. It's just that it's been so long since I went near one, and they're so big and powerful."

"In my experience, the bigger they are, the gentler they tend to be," Glyn said. "And Flicka isn't that big anyway. Let's get her out, and we'll saddle her up."

He opened the door, slipped the halter over the mare's head and led her out into the yard. She was the colour of dark chocolate, her mane and tail were black, and the only white marks on her were the small half-moon on her face and one white hind foot. "Meet your new rider, Flicka. Be gentle with her, girl, she's a bit nervous."

Megan wondered if he was laughing at her, but when she glanced up at him, he did not look as if he was trying to make fun of her.

The mare did not stand as tall as Megan had feared, in fact she could see over her back without stretching. "How tall is she?" she asked curiously.

"She's a shade under fifteen hands, nearly five foot to the withers, that's the base of her neck between her shoulders," he replied." He eyed her appraisingly. "What are you, five foot four or five? About eight stone or so?"

She nodded. "Good guess, I'm five foot four and a half actually, eight stone three."

"You should suit each other well. She'll carry you easily, and she's very gentle and trustworthy."

Megan took a deep breath. Well, that sounded reassuring anyway. Glyn tied the mare to a ring at the side of the stable door and disappeared into the tack room, to reappear a few minutes later with a saddle over one arm and a bridle in his other hand.

He laid the saddle gently on Flicka's back and pulled it back slightly, so it settled into the correct position, then leaned underneath her belly and caught hold of the girth, fastening it loosely. "We'll tighten it up properly after we've put the bridle on," he explained.

Megan watched as he took the bridle from the hook where he'd hung it while he saddled the mare and looped the reins over the horse's neck. Slipping the halter off and holding the headpiece of the bridle in one hand, he used his thumb to encourage her to open her mouth, and he eased in the metal bit. At the same time, he pulled the bridle up over her ears before fastening the throat lash and noseband. He stepped back, holding the reins in one hand so the mare did not move away.

"You see how it's done? It's quite simple once you've done it a couple of times."

She nodded. When Glyn did it, it certainly did look simple. The trouble was, when he stood close to her like this, she found it rather hard to concentrate on anything.

****

Glyn tightened the saddle girth gradually, running his fingers beneath it to make sure it wasn't pinching the horse's sensitive skin. "Okay, I think that's tight enough," he said. "We can always tighten it up again if we need to once you're on." He led the mare into the yard with Megan following closely behind. "It's actually easier for you and the horse if you use a mounting block, but I want you to learn the correct way to mount from the ground. You never know when you may have to dismount when you're riding across country, and there may not always be something you can stand on to get back up."

"I think the idea of me riding across country is a bit ambitious, to say the least," she said, with the glimmer of a smile. She breathed in deeply a couple of times, crammed on her riding hat, fastening the strap, and stepped toward the horse.

Holding the cheek strap of the bridle, Glyn gently put his hand on her shoulder as she stopped and hesitated a moment. "Stand closer to her," he said, trying to take his mind off her closeness to *him*. "That's it. Now take the reins in your left hand and turn to face her tail. Hold the stirrup with your right hand, and put your left foot in. Then just swing your right leg over the saddle. You can hold the front of the saddle with your left hand and put your right hand on the back of the saddle, called the cantle, for balance. Then sit down into the saddle as gently as you can."

"What if she moves while I'm getting on?" she asked, a note of anxiety creeping back into her voice.

"She won't," he assured her. "She's trained to stand still while being mounted, and I'm holding her bridle. I'm right here behind you, I'll make sure you're all right."

She put her foot in the stirrup, as he'd instructed, swung her other leg over and settled into the saddle. The mare stood like a rock, as he knew she would. "How's that?" he asked, "Do you feel comfortable?"

"Yes, I-I think so. I can't reach the stirrups though."

"We can soon sort that out. Just put your leg forward a moment, while I tighten the girth a bit more, then I'll shorten them for you."

Obediently she did as he requested, and he tightened the girth a couple of holes. "She has a habit of blowing herself out when she's been girthed up," he explained. We don't want the saddle slipping once we get moving." He adjusted the stirrup leather, until the stirrup hung just above her ankle, caught hold of her foot and slipped it into the stirrup, then went around to the other side to adjust the right stirrup. "Better?" he asked.

"Yes, fine thanks," she replied, but he noticed she

clung tightly to Flicka's mane.

"Okay. Now you'll need to sit up straight, take a rein in each hand and hold it like this, with your wrists slightly rounded and your thumb on top." He took her hand and placed it gently in the correct position, trying to ignore the heat tingling through him as he touched her skin. She placed her fingers around the other rein, as he showed her.

He walked back toward the loosebox and heard her gasp behind him.

"Aren't you coming with me?" she asked sounding a little panicky.

He laughed softly. "Of course I am. I'm not going to let you go haring off into the countryside by yourself, first time out." He turned back after taking a lead-rein from the rail in front of the loosebox and clipped it onto Flicka's bit.

"Phew. For a moment, I had a scary vision of Flicka galloping off into the hills, with me clinging on for dear life," she said. "Won't you need to get your horse too, then?"

"We won't be going fast, I'm just going to walk with you." Glyn took up a position near Flicka's left shoulder. "Are you ready to move, or do you just want to stand for a little while longer?"

"No, let's do this," she said, her voice sounding just a little nervous.

"Okay then. Squeeze her gently with your heels," he told her. She did as he asked. Nothing happened. Glyn glanced back at her and grinned. "You'll have to press her sides a little harder, I don't think she felt it."

She squeezed harder and this time the mare moved forward a pace or two, then stopped.

"Loosen the reins a bit," he said. "She's not used to a tight rein. If you need something to hang on to, don't worry, it's okay to grab her mane with one hand. It won't hurt her, and it will be much more comfortable for her than if you try to use the reins for support."

Glyn led Flicka at a steady walk into the schooling ring and told Megan not to be too stiff, but to try and go with the movement. It didn't take her long to get used to the swaying rhythmic motion, and by her expression, she had started to relax a little. He sucked in his breath, trying to ignore the effect she had on him. Her hair, flowing from her helmet down her back, glinted in the sunshine, and he could see she wasn't as nervous. Her skin had a warm glow, and she looked so lovely he had to catch his breath and force himself to concentrate on the task in hand. "Are you happy to go along the bridle track a short way?" he asked, hoping his voice did not betray him. "Next time, we can do some work here in the outdoor school, but for your first time I thought it might be nicer for you to just wander along the track. I promise you, if there are any dogs around, Flicka won't turn a hair, she's quite used to them."

"Okay," she said, her voice sounding more confident than when she first mounted the horse. They turned out of the gate, across the yard, and along the drive. After walking a short distance along the lane, they crossed to the other side, through a rider-gate and along the bridleway leading toward some woodland.

"We won't go far today," he told her. "I just want you to get the feel of the horse and the movement. No point in overdoing it and getting stiff." He paused. "Are you all right, you're not still feeling nervous are you? You're really doing fine."

The Matchmaker's Mare

"Yes, actually I'm enjoying it," she said, a hint of surprise in her voice. "Everything looks and even smells so different from the back of a horse. I can see over the hedges. What a wonderful way to see the countryside. I hadn't realised how much more you can see from up here than in a car or on foot."

"Yes, and we're very lucky here, there's plenty of open countryside and bridleways, so there's no need to go onto any major roads."

When they reached the treeline he told her to put a little pressure on the right rein and squeeze Flicka behind the girth with her left heel, and they turned and walked back to the farm.

"Well done," he said on their arrival back at the yard. "You were excellent, we'll make a rider of you yet!" Her smile of pure pleasure made his day. He patted Flicka's neck. "You're a really quick learner," he said. "How do you feel now?"

"Great," she replied, grinning. "I felt much safer than I thought I would, and Flicka was so calm."

"Yes, she's a good old girl," he agreed, giving the mare another piece of carrot from his pocket. "I knew she'd look after you and give you confidence. Now we'd better get you off."

He told her to hold both reins in her left hand. "Place that hand on her neck. Now take both feet out of the stirrups, lean forward, and with your other hand on the front of the saddle swing your right leg over and jump down."

She did as he instructed, and he put his hands lightly around her waist to support her as she dismounted, trying to disregard the waves of desire firing through him at her closeness. Then she turned, with his hands still encircling her waist, and smiled up at him as she unfastened and removed her riding hat. In that moment, all his resolve to keep his distance, at least until his divorce became final, fled, and his feelings for her took over. Instead of stepping back and releasing her, he bent and kissed her on the lips.

She let the helmet slip from her fingers to the ground, placed her arms around his neck, and kissed him back.

Chapter Fourteen

The Kiss

"At last! I had begun to think they would never give in to their feelings."
"Well, you whispered enough hints in their ears."
Rhiannon gave her husband a little nudge. "You are jesting with me now, Sion Sienco."
"No, my love, you know I would never make fun of you."
"Huh!" Rhiannon made a face at the love of her life and tried not to laugh out loud. It would be a shame to spoil this moment she'd worked so hard to bring about.

****

Megan's heart hammered in her chest as Glyn leaned toward her, and his lips touched hers in a gentle kiss, hardly more than a caress, almost as if he were asking permission. She put tentative arms around his neck, trembling, her blood heating in a way she'd never felt before. She closed her eyes, pressing her lips against his, and he pulled her closer, deepening the kiss and holding it for a long, long moment.

Her body trembled with desire, and her heart thumped so hard she thought he must surely hear it. At last, he ended the kiss without letting her go, and looked deep into her eyes as they flicked open again.

"Megan, I've wanted to do that for such a long time." He paused before going on, "I'm very much afraid I'm falling in love with you."

She lowered her gaze from his, and, dropping her arms from around his neck, stepped back a pace. Her mind raced in confusion. This was something she'd fantasized about for so long, despite her promise to herself after her breakup. Now it was happening she could not be sure she could trust her own feelings. She'd told herself she wouldn't allow herself to be hurt again after Richard, and only recently avoided a kiss from Mark. Only this was different. No other man had ever affected her the way Glyn did, just by being near her.

He didn't close the space between them again, but took both her hands in his. "I'm sorry, I didn't mean to be presumptuous, or make you feel uncomfortable. It's just that—" he hesitated. "Megan, you are such a special person. I've grown to care for you more than I could have imagined. I meant what I just said."

She gulped. Her determination not to get involved with another man dissolving like mist in the heat of the morning sun. But what about his wife? Was he still married to her? She would not be a marriage wrecker. If he was still married, whatever her feelings, she could not allow this to go any further. She had to know, and she needed an answer, however painful it might be.

"Glyn are you really sure? I mean..." she hesitated, not quite knowing how to say what was on her mind.

He frowned. "I've never been more sure of anything, why would you doubt it?"

"I wasn't doubting *you*," she said. "Of course I wasn't, but—what about your...wife?"

"We're finished," he told her, his voice heavy. "Anything I might have felt for her died a long time back. I haven't seen Clarissa since she left me over six years ago, and I'm actually waiting for our divorce to be finalised, hopefully any day now."

Megan squeezed his hand, her eyes misty as she gazed up at him. "I'm so sorry, Glyn. But what about Huw? How could she bear to leave him behind?"

"That's something I've often asked myself," he told her. "I just don't know. I wonder if she really wanted a child in the first place. Once the novelty of having a small baby wore off, she seemed to lose interest in him. She'd happily leave him with me while she stayed out all night with her friends. Not that I minded. Huw is the best thing that ever happened to me, but I couldn't understand how she could leave him for hours on end. When he was about two and a half years old, she told me she'd found someone else. Someone who could give her everything she wanted, someone so much more suitable for her and the lifestyle she deserved than I was. She told me since I was so good at looking after Huw, as she put it, I could carry on doing so."

Glyn closed his eyes, frowning, as if recalling painful memories. Megan crept into his arms again and he held her close.

****

After few moments, he took a deep breath and went on, "We got married much too soon, and we were far too young. She was only nineteen and I was two years older, we'd only known each other a short while. Huw was born a year later. I don't think she was really ready to settle down, let alone start a family," he told her. "I can't put all the blame on Clarissa either. I was too involved with the horses and building up my business. I'd just bought the farm in South Wales. It soon became apparent she wasn't happy at the prospect of spending the rest of her life in the Welsh countryside, away from the nightlife and excitement of the city. She and I were so different. Once the initial attraction cooled there was nothing left between us." He sighed. "I thought at first, she'd see sense and come back—if not for me, for the boy. When it became obvious she wasn't going to, I waited the necessary five years and then filed for divorce. By then she was living in France. Unbelievably she wouldn't agree to an amicable settlement, or we could have been divorced sooner."

"I can't believe she could be so unreasonable," Megan said, with a little shake of her head. "If she left you for someone else though, wouldn't that have been grounds to divorce her sooner?"

"I could have cited desertion and adultery, but I didn't like the idea of dragging her name through the divorce courts and, as I said, I thought she might come back and try and make a go of it, for the sake of our son, although any feelings between us were long gone."

He gave a long sigh. "Ironically, the law changed earlier this year. Under this new law, couples can legally separate without either party having to assign blame, and one can apply for a divorce without the consent of the other partner. If this law had gone through sooner, she wouldn't have been able to prolong the process."

Megan shook her head dumbly, unable to find the words to say how she felt. From the sound of it, Glyn's ex had purposely delayed the divorce out of sheer spite. How could anyone be so mean?

"Let's not talk about her anymore," Glyn whispered into her hair. "My marriage was a huge mistake. The only good thing to come from it was Huw. It's in the past now, or soon will be. I didn't mean to tell you how I feel about you until the divorce became final, but having you so close just now—it nearly drove me crazy."

He took her face in both his hands and caressed her lips with his own once more. She responded so fervently his heart raced, and he had to control the urge to draw her even closer, to kiss her breathless and run his hands all over the sweet body pressed against his.

She seemed so vulnerable somehow.

She reminded him of a young, unbroken filly which might spook and run if he was too rough. He knew it would be wrong to ask her to commit to anything just yet, in fact, he wasn't even sure he should have let it get this far.

As if reading his mind she ended the kiss and stepped back a little once more. "Glyn," she said softly, "can we take this slowly? I need to work out my feelings before—" Her voice trailed off.

"Of course," he said. "I promise I'm not going to try to rush you into anything. Once the *decree absolute,* the *Final Order,* comes through, we can see where we want to go with this, although I know beyond any doubt how I feel about you." He glanced at Flicka, still standing patiently beside them. "We'd better unsaddle this old girl and give her a feed," he said, trying to regain his composure with an effort.

Megan nodded and bent to retrieve her helmet. He

took her hand, and they led the horse over to the stable block, together.

Chapter Fifteen

Dreams and Ambitions

"Happy now, cariad?"

"Well, we are not quite there yet, but 'tis a start. These two are meant for each other, I just hope they realise that and do not let anything stop them."

"You must not be so pessimistic my sweet, look at them. They can hardly take their eyes off each other."

Rhiannon nodded, but her voice held a hint of uncertainty when she answered. "True, but Megan wants to take it slow. Nothing wrong with that, she is still a little hesitant about trusting a man again after the way her former boyfriend let her down, and of course Glyn needs to be completely free. I just have a horrible feeling there is something I am not aware of, which might ruin their chances of being happy together." She shrugged. "You are right Sion. I am likely being over-cautious. They do belong together and between us, we have helped them realise it. All they need is another little push, when the time is right."

****

The next few weeks passed in something of a blur. Megan could hardly believe the events of the amazing afternoon when she'd had her first riding lesson with Glyn. Ever since he told her he loved her, she'd felt like an excited teenager embarking on her first romance. He was so different from Richard, and she tried to push that unfortunate part of her past life to the back of her mind.

Nevertheless, something kept her from telling him how much he meant to her, and she could not be sure why. Perhaps she couldn't quite believe that at last she'd found someone who truly loved her. Their relationship seemed so easy and warm she was almost afraid to let herself get in too deep in case it all disintegrated around her. He didn't mention his estranged wife again, and she didn't press the matter. The memories were probably as painful to him as her affair with Richard was to her. Once his divorce finalised, perhaps they would be able to plan for the future—and decide if that future would be together.

****

The weeks passed, bringing with them long, warm summer days. It became routine for Megan to put her riding helmet and a pair of suitable shoes or boots into the SUV in the morning and to stop by at the farm after work, for a riding lesson. She had almost forgotten about her initial nervousness. Flicka was such an obedient and gentle mare, and Glyn so patient and kind an instructor.

She wondered why he had not established a riding school at the farm. He should have no shortage of clients, with his patience and skills as a teacher. When she asked him, Megan caught a barely concealed hint of regret in his voice. He told her in his quiet, matter-of-fact manner, how he had actually qualified as a riding instructor. He worked as an assistant instructor at a large equestrian centre, before purchasing his farm in South Wales and setting up his horse breeding and training business. He had always intended to start a riding school, in addition to breeding and training good quality ponies and horses.

"Clarissa never made any secret of the fact she felt smothered *in the back of beyond* as she put it. When she left us, I decided to give up the idea of a riding school for a few years and start fresh somewhere where I wasn't haunted by bad memories." He passed a hand over his face, as if to try to erase those memories, before continuing. "Much as I love teaching, running a riding school means very long hours, and weekends are especially busy. At the time, I couldn't afford to hire a groom or an assistant instructor, and I needed to be able to give Huw the attention he deserves. When Hafod Farm came up for sale it seemed the ideal place to make a fresh start and expand my breeding and training business. It's not quite so time-consuming as running a riding school."

Megan squeezed his hand to show him she understood. It was so unfair. How many other sacrifices had he been obliged to make since his estranged wife left him and Huw? Megan could understand why he would feel it would take away even more of the precious time he had to be with Huw if he were teaching. She had grown incredibly fond of the boy herself, and enjoyed spending time with him whenever she could, doing her best to pass on some of her skills as a painter. A quick learner, Huw showed great promise for one so young. His main passion, though, like his father, was riding and caring for the horses.

She progressed from being on the lead-rein to walking around the schooling ring by herself, with Glyn giving the occasional instruction. Before long she mastered rising at the trot, which Glyn said was the hardest of all the movements to ride correctly. One evening he told her she was ready to canter. "Keep her going round the school, then just push her into a steady trot. When you're ready, sit still in the saddle and give her a good squeeze with your heels, with your outside leg behind the girth." She did as instructed and the strange, rocking horse movement caught her by surprise. She grabbed hold of a strand of the mare's mane, afraid for a moment she would slip from the saddle. When she got used to the steady rhythm however, she began to enjoy the movement, and relaxed.

"Excellent," Glyn shouted across. "I think you've done enough for tonight. Just ease her back to a walk for a few minutes, and then we'll put her in the paddock." Megan obeyed a little reluctantly. She'd enjoyed herself and couldn't believe she'd actually cantered a horse without feeling nervous. After unsaddling Flicka and laying the saddle on the top rail of the fence, she gave the mare a quick brush, then led her out to where Glyn stood.

"I'm so proud of you *cariad*," he said, holding her close and placing a soft kiss on her lips. "You've conquered your fears, and I think you have the makings of an excellent rider."

"You really think so?" she asked, delighted by his praise, as he walked with her to the paddock. Glyn held the gate while she removed the bridle and let Flikka go free, with a pat and a carrot. "I couldn't have done it without you. You're such a great teacher, I honestly never thought I'd ever ride a horse again, let alone canter—that's nearly a gallop!" They both laughed,

The Matchmaker's Mare

watching the mare roll on her back, snorting and kicking her legs in the air.

"Well, it helps to have a brilliant pupil," he said with a grin. "After you've had a bit more practice and ridden a bit more along the lanes and out in the open, perhaps we'll be able to go for that ride together now, you, me and Huw. What do you say?"

"I'd love to," she said, almost surprising herself. "So long as you two promise not to actually go off at a gallop."

"No way, we'll take it gently. Huw will be so excited. He's been asking me for ages when you'll be able to come riding with us." He squeezed her hand, and she wondered if life could possibly get any better, or if this was all a dream from which she might suddenly awake.

****

Mucking out the looseboxes gave Glyn plenty of time to think. Megan had hit a bit of a nerve when she innocently asked him about the ambition he had long harboured, of starting a riding school at Hafod Farm.

He heaved a bale down from the barn and tossed the fresh, clean straw in a thick layer on the floor of the loosebox he'd just cleaned. Perhaps he should think about making his dream into a reality. There weren't any riding establishments within several miles radius, so he wouldn't have much competition. He already had some cobs and ponies which would be suitable, but he would need to gradually increase his stock of riding ponies. He really wanted to do what he loved most and pass on his knowledge to others.

After paying off the original mortgage on his farm in South Wales, he'd used some of the proceeds from the sale for the deposit on Hafod. He took financial advice and invested what was left of the money from the sale in stocks and shares. They did even better than expected, and he'd managed to put away a fair sum. At present, the proceeds were held in a savings account, with a healthy portion set aside in a trust fund for Huw.

His pony breeding and training business was going well, and since he'd been able to put a large deposit on Hafod, the mortgage was very manageable. Although it would still be tight, he calculated he should have enough savings to enable him to build extra looseboxes, purchase the additional riding ponies and possibly hire a trainee groom.

He also wanted something else, once his divorce became final, which was even dearer to his heart. Megan had never actually spoken the words, but the way she responded when he kissed her, gave him hope she might feel the same way about him as he did about her.

Chapter Sixteen

A Picnic and a Surprise Visitor

Rhiannon settled on the bench outside the cottage and gave a little sigh. "Well, indeed now it does seem to be working out, Sion, does it not. I've never seen Megan look so happy, although she still seems to have a few reservations."

"Reservations?" Sion asked, snuggling up beside her.

"Yes. 'Tis almost as if she is afraid to let herself be happy, in case it is all suddenly snatched away from her."

"Fear not, my love. Glyn seems both kind and considerate. I feel sure he will find a way to convince her to listen to her heart."

Rhiannon gave him an affectionate glance. "Sometimes, for all your foolery, you can be very wise, dearest Sion. I am sure you are right."

****

Megan surprised herself by how much she looked forward to her riding lessons with Glyn. Not only did she enjoy being in the company of the man she'd come to love and respect, she also loved learning to ride the mare she'd also become fond of, and learned to trust.

Every evening after work she would practice trotting and cantering under Glyn's guidance and enjoy short rides in the countryside. Her confidence grew every day. A few weeks after her first canter, she agreed to go for a ride with him and Huw on the following Saturday. They decided to start early, before the sun got too hot, and so they could spend the rest of the day by the river and enjoy a picnic.

On Friday evening, Megan stood before the full-length mirror in her bedroom, trying to decide which shirt to wear. She chose a checked loose-fitting Western style shirt, but as she was about to lay it out ready, a thought came to her. *It's a bit baggy, what about the pale blue one, it's stretchy and comfortable—and will show off your figure.* She looked around quickly, almost expecting to see someone behind her, but of course there was no one there. She shook her head and took a deep breath. Either she had become deranged, or the cottage really did have a ghost. She always seemed to be hearing voices these days.

She put the thought to one side and hung the checked shirt back up. She took the blue one from the hanger and tried it on with her new navy jodhpur-jeans, tucking it in and fastening a narrow black belt around her waist. She looked at herself in the full-length mirror. Hmm, not bad. She'd been right about the shirt; it did look better. Of course she was only going for a horse ride, but she didn't need to look dowdy or scruffy. *And of course you do want to look good for Glyn.* Oh, now she knew for sure she was going crazy, talking back to herself. She sighed. Of course she was crazy. Crazy in love with Glyn Phillips, and she needed to stop trying to kid herself that she wasn't—she was and needed to accept the fact.

Megan rose early next morning to allow plenty of

time to get ready and prepare the picnic food. She'd insisted on providing the food for the picnic and hummed softly as she made egg and cress, smoked salmon, ham and cream cheese, and chicken and mayo sandwiches. She added cold sausage rolls, fresh garden tomatoes, individually wrapped slices of homemade jam sponge cake, and fruit cake, together with some fresh strawberries.

The sun's rays through the kitchen window cast a golden glow across the tiled floor and a blackbird piped its melodious song from a tree just outside. She smiled as she packed the last of the food into a hamper. Today promised to be glorious—in more ways than one.

****

When Megan arrived at Hafod Farm, Huw and Glyn were waiting for her. Huw sat on the chestnut pony, and Glyn stood beside his beautiful mare, Tip-Top. He presented a fine figure, dressed in fawn breeches, long boots, and an open-necked white shirt, with Flicka saddled and bridled ready for her. All three animals had halters beneath their bridles. She smiled at Huw, and Glyn gave her a chaste kiss on the cheek and took the hamper she passed to him, transferring the contents to the saddlebags on both his horse and Flicka.

They rode along the lane, through the gate, and along the track toward the woodland. The ground rose slightly, and they trotted along for a while. Then Glyn asked if she was ready for a canter. Megan nodded and they took off at a steady pace. She gave a happy little laugh, amazed at how comfortable she felt. Because the ground had an upward slope she felt confident Flicka would not go faster than she wished, although Glyn led the group and kept the pace steady.

The track along the edge of the woods gave way to open country, and to one side, a range of mountains towered above them. The nearest peak, Glyn told her, was called Bryn Glas, which meant the *blue hill*. "There are several bridle tracks up the mountainside," he said, and the view is amazing. One day, when you've had a bit more experience, I'll take you up there."

The horses had worked up a gentle sweat, puffing a little after their long canter. They slowed them to a fast walk, skirting the base of the mountains, and eventually, Glyn halted at a grove of trees near the river. The sun made diamond sparkles on the gentle ripples of the surface, and the sound of birdsong in the trees added a melodic accompaniment to the soft rush of the water.

"I think this is a good place for our picnic," Glyn said, and vaulted down from the saddle.

While Huw and Megan unsaddled the horses and tied them to the trees, laying the saddles against the trunks, Glyn busied himself laying out a tablecloth on the grass. He produced several paper plates and cups and even some cartons of fruit juice. "I had thought of bringing some wine," he said, with a mischievous grin, "but I didn't think it would travel too well."

Huw untied a bag from his own saddle and went over to where the horses were tethered.

"I brought some carrots and slices of apples. They want to have a picnic, too."

"Well, I'm glad you thought of them," Glyn said. "They deserve a treat." While Huw busied himself with the horses, Glyn and Megan carried on laying out the feast together. "How did you manage these?" he asked, his eyes twinkling, removing the lids from some small

The Matchmaker's Mare

plastic containers, filled with strawberry jelly and cream. "I'm surprised they haven't turned into a soggy mess after being jolted around in my saddlebag."

"I made the jellies and piped some whipped cream on top and then put them in the freezer," she replied. "I knew they'd thaw slowly as we rode, without getting too soft, and they'll go with the fresh strawberries."

"Great idea," Glyn said, giving her a quick kiss.

When Huw came back, they soon demolished all the sandwiches and cake, topped the jelly and cream with strawberries, and finished the meal off with the fruit juice. They led the horses down to the river for a drink and a splash, then Huw fed them the remainder of their carrots and apple treats.

They spent a long, lazy afternoon in the shade of the trees. They removed the horses' bridles, leaving just their halters, and sat holding the horses' lead ropes so they could chomp on the grass. Huw chattered away, full of the things he'd been up to with Seren. Megan made an effort to pay him attention and share his enthusiasm, but her gaze kept wandering to Glyn. Every time her eyes met his, he smiled at her with that lazy grin of his, and she felt herself blush.

After a while, when Huw had run out of steam, Glyn related the sad tale of Gelert, the favourite hound of Prince Llewelyn. Megan never tired of hearing his voice, and the way he told a story made the old legend come to life.

"Llewelyn returned from a hunt," he began. "He'd left his favourite hound, Gelert to guard his baby son. The hound ran to greet his master, covered with blood. Llewelyn charged through the door of his castle and saw the baby's cradle overturned and no sign of the child. In grief and anger, believing his beloved dog had killed his little son, he ran the animal through with his sword, only to be startled by the sound of a baby crying. He found the child beneath his cradle, and nearby, the body of a wolf the courageous hound had slain. Those were the days when wolves still roamed Britain," he went on. "Overcome with remorse, Llewelyn buried the dog with great ceremony. Despite making what amends he could, he continued to hear the dog's dying yelps in his mind, and it's said he never smiled again."

"Oh, how sad," Megan said. "Are all Welsh legends so tragic, don't you know any that are a bit more cheerful?"

"Yes, of course," he replied. "Did you know we had a Welsh Robin Hood?"

"You're joking," she said thinking he was winding her up.

"No, really. His name was Twm Sion Cati. He roamed west and mid-Wales, robbing the rich, but somehow forgetting the bit about giving to the poor. He's depicted as a rather likeable rogue. In fact, I believe they made a television series about him, back in the '70s."

"Thanks for sharing that one, Gwyn," Megan said. These old legends are fascinating. How do you know so much about them?"

"Oh, we learnt a lot of them when I was at school. There are many of the old folk tales in a very famous book *The Mabinogion*. I have a copy at home. I'll lend it to you if you like."

"I'd like that very much." Megan felt a warm glow. Who knew a Welsh horse dealer would have such an interest in ancient Welsh literature? Glyn had kept his promise to let her take things at her own pace, and never asked for more than a gentle embrace and kiss. The more they were together, the more she felt they were absolutely right for each other, and realised not all men were like Richard. Tonight, when Huw was in bed and they were alone, she would pluck up the courage to tell him how much she loved him. How she wanted to be with him when he was finally free.

****

Eventually, the sun dipped below the hills. They gathered up the remains of the picnic, putting the empty paper plates and cups, together with the folded-up tablecloth, into Glyn's saddlebags.

They rode home at a leisurely pace, leaving the reins loose and letting the horses pick their own way through the trees. They kept to a gentle trot along the track, slowing to a walk when it sloped downhill, until they came to the lane leading to Hafod Farm. Megan rode alongside Glyn, and Huw rode his pony ahead of them. Glyn moved Tip-Top closer to Flicka and took hold of Megan's hand.

She looked across at him, unable to repress her happiness. "Thank you," she said. "This has been an amazing day. I can't remember when I enjoyed myself so much."

"Neither can I," he told her. "I've loved having you with us, and I think Huw's enjoyed today as much as I have." He smiled down at her, and although no more words were spoken, she felt something special had passed between them.

"We'll let them walk home," Glyn said, raising his voice so Huw, who had urged Seren into a trot again, could hear, "to make sure they get back cool. Then we can just brush them down, give them a quick feed and turn them straight out into the paddocks."

A few minutes later, he glanced up at the sky, which was now darkening, where minutes before it had been clear blue. "Uh-oh, looks like a storm's gathering," he said. "On second thoughts, perhaps we'd better jog on a bit, before the rain comes."

Until then, she hadn't noticed the clouds bubbling up, or the slight breeze now rustling through the trees. As they approached the farm, the gathering storm clouds had already caused the atmosphere to chill. To her surprise, Megan noticed a large, flashy-looking car parked outside the house. She gave Glyn a questioning look, but he seemed as surprised as she was. He dismounted to open the gate and led his horse toward the car. At the same time, the car door opened and a tall, blonde woman, possibly two or three years older than Megan, stepped out. Impeccably dressed in a pale green suit, and four-inch heels, she removed her fashionable sunglasses, and her ruby-painted lips formed a stiff smile as Huw jumped down from his pony.

By now Megan had also dismounted, and the woman turned, her thin lips forming a poor semblance of a smile. "Glyn, aren't you going to introduce me to—" she looked down her nose at Megan with a haughty expression, "your *friend*?"

Glyn looked distinctly uncomfortable, and his face registered something like shock. "Oh, um, yes, of course. This is Megan Johnson. She's a good friend and I've been teaching her to ride. Megan…this is—er—" his voice trailed off and he seemed reluctant to finish the sentence.

"Oh, spit it out, Glyn," the woman said, her tone even colder than the icy fingers which suddenly traced themselves up and down Megan's spine. She stepped closer to Glyn and laid a possessive hand on his arm for a moment before stating, "Miss Johnson, I'm Clarissa Phillips—Glyn's wife."

Thunder rumbled in the distance. Megan shivered as the first heavy spots of rain fell and inky dark clouds drove across the sky. Her stomach knotted and she leaned against Flicka's warm flank, feeling weak, as if someone had punched her in the stomach and her knees were about to give way. "G—good evening," she stammered, not knowing what else to say.

The woman gave a disdainful nod and turned back to Glyn. She did not offer her hand, and neither did Megan. She wished she were anywhere but standing there with the rain blowing into her face, the other woman's haughty glare making her feel like a small child caught stealing a chocolate bar. She needed to get away. The emotions swirling around in her head threatened to overwhelm her, and she was afraid she'd embarrass herself and say something she regretted if she stayed any longer.

"I'm—I'm afraid I'll have to go now," she said at last, avoiding eye contact with Glyn and looking directly at Huw. "Huw, would you mind seeing to Flicka for me, I'm sorry I don't have time to stay and unsaddle her myself."

Huw nodded. "All right, Megan," he said in a low voice, looking from her to his mother with a confused expression on his face. Glyn had said Clarissa left when he was only two and a half. No wonder he looked confused. It must be just registering in the boy's mind this might be his mother.

Aware of Clarissa's hostile glare as she did so, Megan gave him a quick hug. He looked as if he needed one. What the heck! Clarissa might be Glyn's wife, but Megan had done nothing to be ashamed of and she'd be damned if she'd let the woman lord it over her.

She glanced briefly toward the two adults, then walked over to her vehicle. She slid into the driver's seat and drove out of the yard without a backward glance, trying to ignore the salty taste of tears in her mouth and clouding her vision. The rain, falling in earnest now, lashed against the windscreen as if in sympathy, making the visibility even worse. She could only give thanks there were no other drivers on the narrow country lane that evening.

Once indoors, she sank into the nearest chair biting back the scalding tears that burned her eyes, threatening to fall in earnest. Crying would not solve anything. She wasn't a child. Lightning flashed at the windows, and she drew the curtains without bothering to switch on the light. The thunder rumbled overhead, and she shivered, realising how her damp shirt clung to her and knowing she really ought to change. She made her way to her bedroom, going over the events of the last half hour in her mind.

So that was his wife. Despite Glyn's assertion he was waiting for their divorce to be finalised, Clarissa obviously still considered herself married to him. Had he been lying through his teeth all this time?

Why had she let herself get so involved? She should have known it was too good to be true.

The day which had seemed so wonderful now felt

tainted. All she could think of was the scorn in Clarissa's eyes as she stood there in her elegant, tailored suit, eyeing her as if she were some unkempt, guileless teenager. No doubt she'd put two and two together and made a dozen. Well, whatever the other woman thought, Megan was no homewrecker. She had to face facts though. Although Glyn seemed shocked to see Clarissa, he'd introduced Megan as a 'good friend'! *A good friend*—after telling her how much he loved her—and Clarissa had not acted as if they were on the verge of divorce. She gave a ragged sigh. Even if Glyn had not been lying to her, she could never hope to compete with someone as glamorous as that woman. Clarissa was beautiful and sophisticated and gave the impression of someone who was used to getting what she wanted. If that was to get back with Glyn, what earthly chance did *she* have of competing with her?

****

Glyn watched Megan drive away and passed his hand over his face. He drew in a deep breath. The look of betrayal in her eyes was not something he could just brush away. She must have felt everything he'd told her had been a lie, and the happiness they'd shared for the last couple of months meant nothing to him. He fought the urge to drive after her, but he couldn't just leave Huw—or the horses—and besides it might be better to give her some space. He'd call her when he'd spoken to Clarissa and found out the reason for her unexpected return.

When she'd left him, she made it very plain she wanted a new life for herself. She left his emails unanswered, and even the few letters he'd written were returned unopened. The divorce correspondence had been handled by their respective solicitors acting as intermediaries.

Now here she was, dressed like something out of a fashion magazine, and acting as if she'd just been away for a week or two on business. He tried to read her face for answers. Did she regret leaving them six years ago?

"You might have given me some warning you intended coming to see me—"

"What, so you could make sure your girlfriend wasn't around? Anyway, I came to see my son as well as you."

"Dad?" Glyn looked down and his heart went out to the boy, who looked shocked and confused. As shocked and confused as he felt himself, in fact.

Huw turned to look at Clarissa. "Are—are you my mother?"

"Of course, I am. I've been away for a while but I'm back now. You've certainly shot up since I last saw you. You were only a toddler then, you know. Aren't you going to give me a hug?"

Huw backed toward Glyn again, and he put an arm around the child's shoulder.

"Clarissa, you can't turn up out of nowhere, after all this time, and expect him to remember you just like that."

She tossed back her perfectly styled hair and for a moment seemed to lose a little of her composure. Glyn had to admit while she might be six years older than when he last saw her, she'd lost none of her attractiveness. Tall, blonde and blue-eyed, with a figure like a cover model, she looked every inch the beauty he'd been so infatuated with when they first met. He'd married the woman a few weeks after they were introduced, without stopping to think whether they were really suited.

"I suppose it might take a little time," she confessed. "He'll come round. Aren't you going to invite me into the house, Glyn? I want to see what sort of place you've got here, and, in case you hadn't noticed, it's raining."

"I'm afraid you'll have to wait until we've seen to the horses," he told her, still in something of a daze.

"Can't they wait? Isn't it more important for us to talk?"

"Well…it's been six years, Clarissa. A few more minutes won't make any difference." He turned back to the three horses. "I'm sorry, but no, they can't wait. They need to be unsaddled, rubbed down and fed, before they get too wet and cold. We can talk as soon as they're tended to."

"I suppose I'll just have to wait in the car then."

Glyn inclined his head without replying, and he and Huw led the horses across the yard to the stable block. As they approached, Evan came out from one of the outbuildings.

"You've seen your visitor then, Glyn?"

"Yes," he said. "She's in the yard in her car, waiting for me."

Evan took the reins of all three horses. "Better go and talk to her then, Boss. I'll see to these three."

"Thanks," Glyn said, "I'd really appreciate that." He put his arm around Huw's shoulder again and walked with the boy back toward the house.

At the very least, Clarissa owed him some answers.

Chapter Seventeen

A Decision

"What are we going to do now Sion, I cannot bear to see her so unhappy—just as I thought we had brought them together at last and everything was going to work out. What can we do to make this right again?" Rhiannon sighed deeply, a sound that echoed the wind in the trees behind the house.

"No good askin' me, cariad, you're the matchmaker." Sion moved closer to her and placed a comforting arm around her shoulder "But you weren't to know his wife would come back to him after deserting him for so long."

"I know. Perhaps I should have seen this coming, though. It was always a possibility."

"Now, Rhiannon, there is no point blamin' yourself. We must just put our heads together an' see if there is a way we can sort this out."

Rhiannon sighed again. "Perhaps you are right Sion, but I declare I can see no way of making this right, indeed I cannot. I suppose all we can do at present is try to make things as easy for her as we can."

****

The thunder passed, and the rain cleared by the morning. Megan prepared a light breakfast which she only picked at. Her mind was still in a state of

The Matchmaker's Mare

confusion. She did not even feel up to going to the little chapel she'd been in the habit of attending. The sound of the chapel bells ringing out across the valley seemed to chide her for being so pathetic. Her mobile *beeped* and when she checked there was a text message and a voice message from Glyn. They both said the same thing. *Megan, please call me when you get this, we need to talk.* She sighed, closing her phone. Having gone over and over the previous day's events in her mind, it was clear she needed to know where she stood. Perhaps she'd misconstrued the situation. Just because Clarissa breezed back into his life and acted as if they were still married didn't necessarily mean he was happy about it and wanted to get back with her—did it? However, she couldn't face talking to him at the moment, She needed to clear her head first.

After listlessly pottering around for a while, she decided to walk across the fields to the village. The Post Office opened for a few hours on a Sunday morning, and she bought a magazine for something to do, not because she wanted something to read. When she returned, she saw a car parked outside the cottage. She recognised it immediately as the classy model belonging to Clarissa Phillips. Her heart lurched, and she wondered if Glyn was with her. However, as soon as she reached the car, the door opened and Clarissa stepped out, and it was apparent she was alone.

"Well, good morning," the woman said, her tone sarcastic. "I've been waiting for ten minutes for you to put in an appearance."

"I'm sorry?" Megan said, not feeling the slightest bit apologetic. Why should she, especially as Clarissa Phillips had arrived unannounced. "I went across the fields to the Post Office. I wasn't expecting a visitor."

"No? Well, I came to return this. You left it at Hafod Farm."

She handed Megan a bright red sweater, with the air of someone handling something they found at the bottom of a waste bin. Megan recognised it as one she'd taken down to the farm in case the weather turned chilly. She must have left it in the hayshed or the tack room, or perhaps Glyn had taken it up to the house. She could see by the expression on the woman's face she'd drawn her own conclusions as to Megan's relationship with her husband.

"Thank you," she said, not bothering to keep the coolness out of her voice and taking the sweater from her. She wondered why Glyn hadn't brought it back himself, it seemed strange he should send his wife. The woman's next words answered her unspoken question though. "Glyn doesn't know I'm here. I got your address from someone in the village. I found your sweater before he could hide it or get rid of it. I don't know what you and my husband have been getting up to, but it's over. I don't intend to let any little country girl steal my husband now we're back together."

Megan stared at her aghast.

"How dare you come to my property, insult me, and accuse me of husband stealing? You're the one who left him to bring up your child alone. You abandoned your son when he was just a couple of years old and needed you most. You should be ashamed of yourself." She thought she saw a tinge of crimson creep over Clarissa's face beneath the immaculately applied make-up.

The next moment, it was replaced by a scowl. "I'm

warning you—stay away from Hafod Farm and my husband if you know what's good for you," she spat out. Before Megan could reply, she turned and went back to the car, backing it down the narrow drive and out onto the lane, leaving Megan staring after her, open-mouthed.

So, it seemed Clarissa had reached a reconciliation with Glyn. Perhaps she'd managed to persuade him to withdraw the divorce petition. From what little Megan knew of divorce law, it could be stopped before the *decree absolute* or *Final Order* was issued, if both parties were agreeable.

Had they even been in the process of divorcing at all? Was everything Glyn told her a lie? He'd made it seem as if he wanted nothing more to do with Clarissa, and she had cut ties with him and the boy. Perhaps he'd decided to give their marriage a second chance for the sake of their son. Something had obviously changed, and Clarissa made it very clear no one would be allowed to get between her and her husband now.

What a fool she'd been. She should never have let herself think she had any chance for happiness with Glyn. At first it had been convenient to just assume his wife had died. When he finally told her Clarissa was still very much alive, she'd been happy to accept his explanation that they were irreconcilably separated and soon to be divorced. More fool her, falling for the oldest lie in the book. First Richard, then Mark—and now Glyn. The misery engulfing her now morphed into something approaching anger. It seemed she was fated to attract men who proved completely false, unsuitable, or untrustworthy. Well, no more. In future, she'd treat all men with the contempt they deserved. The idea did not make her feel any better though. It was her own fault. She'd vowed not to risk her heart again, and she'd done just the opposite, only this time it felt much worse than it had with Richard. *Much* worse.

She went inside the cottage, flinging the sweater onto a nearby chair, and made herself a cup of tea to try to calm her nerves. Her encounter with Clarissa Phillips had unsettled her more than she cared to admit.

She heaved a sigh, and came to an abrupt decision. She needed to get away, otherwise she'd drive herself mad mooning over Glyn Philips and comparing herself to his glamorous wife. How could she ever have thought she might have a future with him? She'd been such an idiot. She needed to take some time out for herself and try to blot him out of her mind. She checked her watch—10:45 a.m.

Picking up her phone, she tapped the veterinary practice manager's home number.

"I'm really sorry to bother you at home on a Sunday, but something's come up. I was wondering if I could take a couple of days unpaid leave? I'm sorry it's such short notice, and I know I haven't really been here long enough for much leave, but there's a bit of a family emergency—"

She hated having to tell a white lie, but she didn't know what else to say. She had to get away from there, to go somewhere and collect her thoughts, decide what to do next. Perhaps a little time away from Glyn Phillips would help her distance herself from him enough to quell the longing she felt whenever she thought of him and his lilting Welsh accent. She needed to banish the memories of those dark brown eyes gazing into hers, and the way he'd looked at her sometimes, when they were alone together. How he would take her hand, as they told each other about their day, and a thousand other little things she loved about him.

"Well," Mike Evans' voice came down the line, bringing her back to reality, "I suppose you have earned a break. You haven't had so much as a day's annual leave all summer. We're not so busy at the moment, and Mair can cope for a few days without you. Catrin and Bethan will always help out if it does get a bit busier. When did you want to start your leave?"

"I was hoping I could start it tomorrow," she said, her voice a little uncertain, "if that would be all right."

She waited when there was a short pause before Mike replied, "No problem, Megan. I'll block the next five days in as your annual leave. Let me know if you need any more time. Was there anything else?"

"No, thank you. I appreciate it, and again, I'm sorry for the short notice."

"That's fine," he said. "I hope the emergency is sorted out soon."

"Thanks," she took a deep breath and ended the call. She had no idea where she would go. She had no close family and seemed to have lost touch with most of her friends in London. Oh well, she would just drive and see where the road led her. She noted another message from Glyn, asking her to call him back. She couldn't face speaking to him until she'd had some time to sort things out in her mind and was able to talk calmly. She knew if she spoke to him now she'd be unable to talk lucidly, especially if he wanted to confirm he was getting back with Clarissa.. Taking a deep breath, she texted a quick message: "*I need to be away for a while. I'll give you a call when I get back,"* before thrusting the phone back into the pocket of her jeans.

She packed a small suitcase and flung it in the back of the SUV. She still wasn't sure where she would go, she just knew she wanted to get as far away from Pentrebont and its memories as she could.

She headed south. She'd cross the Severn Bridge into England and stop overnight at a guesthouse in Bristol. She could stay somewhere on the coast for a few days, perhaps, or maybe find a small country hotel somewhere. She just wanted to get away and try and make sense of the turmoil in her mind. After driving for a couple of hours, she found a quaint little country pub and stopped for lunch. She seated herself at a table in a quiet corner, near a window looking out onto spacious lawns. She picked at her pub lunch, glad there weren't many other people there.

She went over the past few months, the cottage, her job at the vets—and always she came back to Glyn. He was constantly there at the back of her mind, and try as she would, she could never quite get the image of him to fade, or the ache in her heart to go away. He'd seemed so trustworthy and kind and helped her overcome her fear of riding a horse. That, at least, was something to be grateful for. She almost smiled, as she recalled the day of the picnic: The aroma of the summer blossoms mingling with the scent of the warm horse. The thud of the horses' hooves on the grassy track as they trotted through the woods, and the feel of the soft skin of the mare when she stroked her neck. The moment when Huw sprinted ahead on Seren, and Glyn reached across and took her hand. For a while, they'd ridden together holding hands, and she felt transported to another time, and a world in which only he and she existed. Well, that bubble had soon burst, hadn't it?

She brought her thoughts back to the present with an effort. She squared her shoulders and came to a decision. She could either spend the entire week brooding, or she could make use of her time off. Time was too precious to waste it moping over a man. With that, came another notion. She'd believed she needed some space, space away from Glyn Phillips to distance herself from him physically and mentally. With something of a shock, she realised she was actually running away—running not only from him, but from the woman who deserted her husband and small son. The same woman who'd turned up out of the blue and had the nerve to threaten her.

Another thought struck her. She only had Clarissa's word she and Glyn were back together. After all, she hadn't given Glyn chance to confirm or deny it had she? She grimaced inwardly. She hated confrontation. So what? What was Clarissa going to do to her if she went back to Hafod Farm to get at the truth? Instead of running away, she should be confronting them both. They owed her an explanation. If Clarissa *was* back to stay, she needed to know for sure, so she could move on with her life, hard though it might be.

She paid her bill, exchanged a few pleasantries with the young woman who'd served her, and, once behind the wheel, turned the car around and headed back in the direction of Pentrebont and home.

****

"Megan, please get back to me when you get this.

We really need to talk."

The message flashed up: *It has not been possible to connect your call. Please try again later.* Glyn sighed. How many times had he called her? He supposed he couldn't blame Megan for not taking his calls. Clarissa's sudden appearance must have been as much of a shock for her as it was to him, if not more, but he wished she'd give him the chance to explain. Perhaps there was no signal where she was—or was he just clutching at straws? Of course she *had* messaged him to say she was going away, and that she would call him, but she'd not said where she was going, or for how long.

He could call the surgery on Monday, if he still couldn't get hold of her. At least someone there might be able to tell him when she was likely to return, and he could only hope she'd keep to her promise and call him when she was back home.

Chapter Eighteen

A Plea in the Night

"This is becoming serious, Sion. We have to get them back together again, but 'tis going to take more than a fruit crumble to fix things this time. She will not even talk to him."

"I think you are right Rhiannon my sweet, so what are you proposin' to do about it?"

"I really do not know at the moment, Sion." Rhiannon drifted around the room and rearranged some ornaments on the mantle shelf and the top of the bookcase, then put them back in their original positions again.

"Well, I might have an idea," Sion stated, *"but we need to time it right—and we can't do anythin' until Megan gets back."*

"Indeed! And I am not sure about your ideas, Sion Sienco. It might be best if you leave it to me." She frowned. *"Talking about plans, I think 'tis time you worked out a plan to get my pony back. I miss her. She has been with me even longer than you have. I will never find another like her. She is very special."*

Sion floated up from the comfortable window seat where he'd been reclining and glided across to Rhiannon wrapping his arms around her and nuzzling her hair. "Well why not think of a way of getting her back yourself? She is your pony, and you were always the clever one."

"Hark to yourself! You were the one who left her with Glyn Phillips for a start—just to annoy me."

"Well, you annoyed me first."

"Huh! I only said you should be careful not to let your presence be suspected when you went snooping around the farm just after Megan came to live at the cottage. You know how most mortals feel about us."

Sion jerked back. "You were the one who said Glyn looked lonely. So what did you think I would do? Perhaps you expected me to walk up to the front door and say 'Excuse me, my wife is a matchmakin' spirit. She asked me to come and find out if you might be needin' someone to help you find a new wife, and to see if you are goin' to be spooked if we come to visit now and then'." He pursed his lips. "Anyway, I only meant it as a prank," he said. "I thought the mare would come back herself eventually. How was I to know she and the boy would take to each other?"

"You were not thinking at all though, were you Sion my love."

"Well now, I did try to set things up so you can get your darned pony back. Did I not arrange things so Glyn's mare would have a foal the boy can have when it is old enough?"

"We made it happen together Sion Sienco, and it has not stopped him hanging on to the pony has it? If I did not care for you so much, I could get really vexed with you I could, and all these silly tricks you keep playing."

"Aw, come on tell the truth. It's what makes the afterlife interestin'. ...Come now, admit it. You would

be bored out of your mind if I did not keep you on your toes all the time."

Rhiannon sighed. "Yes, well that is as maybe. You can sort out that mess later. First, we have to think about what we can do to get Megan and Glyn back together again."

****

The journey back to Wales seemed interminable, the roads heaving with late holiday makers. At times traffic slowed to a crawl, and Megan was held up in a couple of traffic jams for what seemed an eternity each time.

By the time she reached Ty Gwyn the evening was drawing in. Once inside the cottage, she left her case in the hall by the stairs. She would unpack later. She needed a cup of tea. While the kettle boiled, she turned on the television. Not that she wanted to watch anything in particular, but it would stop her thinking too much. She didn't *want* to think, because she knew her mind would torment her with ideas about what might have been. Now she was back in the cottage it was even harder to prevent Glyn Phillips and his seeming duplicity from invading her mind.

After a light supper she decided, a little reluctantly, to check her phone and make sure there were no urgent emails. She'd left it on 'silent' and there was always the possibility there might be a message from one of the girls at the surgery.

She was not surprised to find there was another text message from Glyn. *Please call me as soon as you can when you get back. I need to talk to you.* She pursed her lips. She would phone him tomorrow and arrange a meeting. If he could look her in the eyes and tell her she meant nothing to him and he wanted to mend his marriage, at least she would have closure. She could try to get on with her life.

There were no other messages, nor had she expected there to be. About to open the inbox of her Email account, she started when the mobile's call tone sounded. When she saw the name of the caller she nearly hit 'dismiss'. She'd told him she would get back to him. He wouldn't be aware she'd returned home already, and he could wait until the morning. However, from somewhere in the back of her mind came the thought: *Just answer. He's not texting you this time, perhaps there's a reason.*

She hesitated. Perhaps old Jack had fallen ill. She couldn't ignore a call for help for an animal. She let it ring for a while longer, then hit 'reply'.

She took a deep breath. "Hello," she said, "I've just got home, and I'm tired. Is this something you can leave until tomorrow? Unless it's a matter of life or death I'm hanging up."

"Megan, oh Megan you're home, thank goodness. Please *don't* hang up, I'm sorry to bother you, but this is an emergency." His voice sounded so strained, Megan felt an immediate wave of sympathy, followed by a surge of doubt. Was this just a ploy to get her to talk to him? Was it a call borne out of guilt? After all, if Clarissa was to believed, he'd lied to her about his feelings for his estranged wife—and what possible emergency could there be for him to need her help?

"What is it, Glyn," she asked, trying to keep her voice calm, aware of the hammering of her heart. "I've had a long drive and, as I said, I'm tired."

****

The Matchmaker's Mare

Glyn stood in the yard and once more called up Megan's number on his phone.

"Please Megan, please pick up this time. I really need you."

The phone seemed to ring forever.

"Come *on* Megan, *please.*"

The relief, when she eventually answered and he heard her voice at the other end, washed over him like a tidal wave. He'd driven to her cottage late that morning in the hope she might still be there and would allow him to try to explain the situation she seemed to have misinterpreted. Her car wasn't there, and her message had given no indication of when she expected to return. He had no way of knowing if she'd be back by now, or if she'd respond to his call, but he had to try. She was the only person he could think of who might be able to help and somehow, he had to get through to her.

"I-I'm sorry Megan. I didn't know who else to contact. It's Huw, you see. He's run away."

****

Megan felt as if her legs had been kicked from under her, the misery she already felt compounded by Glyn's statement. Her heart thudded even more wildly against her chest. This couldn't be true. Why would Huw do something like that? "What do you mean, he's run away?" she repeated dumbly.

"He's gone off on that pony of his—"

"You're sure he hasn't just gone for an evening ride?"

"Not at this time of night. Besides, he left a note, and Evan saw him take off." The words came out in a rush, far removed from Glyn's usual, easy way of talking. "Evan came over specially, although it's

Sunday, to mend a broken fence, and didn't finish until late. I was in the house doing some paperwork when he rushed in and said he saw Huw as he went across the yard on the pony. He shouted after him and tried to stop him, but he and Seren took off at a gallop. I found the note on his bed. It said he's running away and is going to hide on Bryn Glas—and he hasn't got his phone with him, either."

"What? Why? Never mind." Her mind raced. She could hear the strain in Glyn's voice. The young boy was alone on his pony on the mountain, and with night falling—no wonder he was worried.

"I've got to go after him, bring him back before he has an accident. Thing is, my pick-up seems to have broken down. It was all right this morning—and Evan's van has a flat tyre."

"What? Doesn't he have a spare?"

"Yes, usually, but somehow it appears to have gone missing. Some coincidence. He swears it was in the van this morning. It would happen now. Megan, I'm sorry to ask, but I'm really worried. If it there was enough light I'd take Tip-Top, but it's getting late. I can't risk the horse losing her footing on the mountain when it's dark, and maybe breaking a leg—"

"All right, I'll be there as soon as I can," Megan assured him, trying to regain her composure. "Just call me back if he should turn up before I get there."

****

She slipped on a jacket against the night air, grabbed her torch, and made for the door. What on Earth was going on at Hafod Farm? First Huw running off on his pony, then both Glyn and Evan having problems with their vehicles at the same time—and what about Clarissa? Glyn hadn't mentioned her. She probably didn't want to scratch her expensive car by driving all over the Welsh mountains, but surely even Clarissa wouldn't put that before her own son's safety? Did Glyn know Clarissa had warned her to stay away from Hafod Farm? To hell with it, Huw might be in danger, and Glyn had asked for her help. There was no time to ponder on any of this. Unless Glyn had been lying to her about Huw running away, which she found hard to believe. Despite everything, finding his son was more important than speculating about Clarissa.

She hated the idea of the youngster riding alone at night. She knew the mist could come down very suddenly in these mountains, and he could easily get lost. Anything could happen. He could slip from the pony's back if she stumbled and fall down the mountainside. She shuddered. Best not to think about the worst-case scenario and concentrate on finding the lad.

She put her foot down on the accelerator and drove at a speed she would not normally have contemplated on these narrow country roads. She prayed nothing was coming the other way, or that a rabbit or badger would not suddenly dash across the road.

As she drove through the open gate of Hafod Farm, she noticed Clarissa's car did not seem to be in the yard, but this was not the time to ask the questions crowding her mind. She assumed Clarissa had probably put her car in one of the outbuildings, or, more likely, Glyn's garage next to the house. She didn't seem the type to allow it to get dirty or wet by leaving it out in the open.

Evan and Glyn were waiting in the yard, with the

young dog, Jack. She noted with relief, along with some surprise, Clarissa wasn't with them. They scrambled into the vehicle as Megan held open the door, and then opened the rear door for Jack to jump in.

Evan, in the back seat, pointed in the direction of the mountain Glyn had called Bryn Glas. "That way, to the mountain, that's where he was going, see."

"He'll have gone across the fields along the bridle path. We'll have to turn off at the bottom of the lane and follow the road around to the forestry track," Glyn put in. We'll be able to drive part of the way up the mountain but only for a short distance."

Megan followed his directions, and they eventually turned into the forest and drove along the rough forestry road.

"These mountain paths can be dangerous," Glyn said. "I've told him he's not to ride there by himself, not even in broad daylight." Megan caught a catch in his voice as he went on, "If he should fall off in the dark, or if the pony should slip—"

"Don't worry, we'll find him," she assured him, although he'd echoed her own fears. "It's still not quite dark, and with any luck, Jack will soon pick up his scent."

There was, indeed, still enough light for them to see the rough mountain path ahead of them. She turned off the forestry track and slowed down, manoeuvring the vehicle along the narrow path twisting up the mountain. Eventually, however, they came to a place where the track levelled out and divided in two and then branched off again, making three different directions boy and pony could have taken. Megan halted the vehicle and all three got out and shone their torches on the stony ground. The now fading light made it difficult to see any hoofmarks. Even if it had been broad daylight, Huw's pony wasn't shod, and the paths were crisscrossed with the hoofmarks of the myriad semi-wild mountain ponies.

"I suggest we leave the vehicle here with Megan. I can take Jack and go this way." Glyn gestured to the middle track which led upward and straight ahead. "Evan, perhaps you can take the left-hand fork."

"No problem," Evan said turning in the direction Glyn indicated.

"I'm not staying here. It makes more sense if the three of us search," Megan put in, switching off her torch to save the battery. She swallowed hard, trying to damp down the feeling of panic at the idea of being on the mountain with dark rapidly falling. "I'm assuming Huw might have taken any of these three tracks?"

Glyn's brow furrowed as he gazed steadily at her. "Yes. All three paths are fairly safe in the daylight, for anyone who knows them, but at night it's a different matter, that's why I'm so worried. I really don't like the idea of you going off by yourself though, especially when you don't know the mountain. It's best you stay here and leave Evan and me to look for Huw."

"No, I want to search, too. It's common sense for us each to take one of these paths." She could see Glyn was not happy about her suggestion, but at last, he let out a sharp breath.

"We're just wasting time standing here arguing. As I said, I don't like the idea of you walking alone on the mountain when you don't know these paths."

"Then why don't I take Jack?"

Glyn still looked uncertain. "Well, I suppose it's

better than you being completely by yourself, but I don't want you putting yourself in any danger."

"I'll be fine," she assured him, moving to the back of the SUV to let the dog out. "It's still not quite dark yet, and I'm quite used to walking over rough terrain." It wasn't entirely true, although she had done a fair bit of walking since she'd lived here, but Glyn didn't need to know that.

"Just promise me you'll call me at once if there's the slightest problem or you think the going is getting too difficult—or dangerous."

She nodded. Glyn looked at his watch. "Whoever comes across him, can let the others know on their mobile. And we'll call each other in an hour's time if no one's found him by then."

Evan waved a hand in acknowledgement and started off along the track leading upwards.

"Megan, I can't tell you how grateful I am for your help." Glyn started. "I've tried calling you since—"

She held up a hand to silence him. "We need to find Huw. We can talk after."

"Of course." His voice had a despondent edge to it she'd never heard before. "We'll find him," she said again, noting the expression of anguish in his eyes, obvious despite the rapidly fading light.

"Jack, go with Megan," Glyn said to the dog. "Take care, Megan, and don't take any risks. Stick close to Jack. He knows these tracks as well as I do."

He sounded concerned, as if he did care something for her after all. She dismissed the thought, with a shake of her head. They were losing precious time. Every second counted with the darkness falling swiftly now. Her mind raced with fear for the boy and imaginings of all the accidents that could befall him.

"All right, I'll call you if I find him."

"Megan—"

About to take the middle track, she stopped and inclined her head toward him.

"Remember what I said, please—be careful."

"All right, don't worry about me. Let's just find that son of yours."

Chapter Nineteen

A Mountain Search

A little earlier the same evening: a wisp of mist swirled around like a miniature tornado, before settling into the form of Rhiannon. "Sion, we have to go—now. The boy might be in trouble. 'Tis not the way I would have wished it, but we can salvage this situation and turn it to our advantage if we hurry."

"What do you mean, turn it to our advantage? Rhiannon, cariad, this is serious. It is not somethin' to take lightly."

Rhiannon had glared at him, then sighed, her tone anxious. "I know that, Sion. Trust me, you know I will not let anything bad happen. Now, while I am making sure it does not, you can do something to help me bring Glyn and Megan back together. We have not set foot in the mountains since that terrible night so long ago, and I dread even thinking about it, but this is an emergency. However hard it is to contemplate venturing into the mountains again, we have to go to Bryn Glas. First though, Sion, my love—we both know you can charm animals, how are you with horseless carriages?"

****

Megan began the steep ascent, Jack at her heels, and turned on her torch again, not wanting to miss her footing in the half-light. She swallowed hard. Despite her insistence on helping to search, she really didn't like being out after dark and the light had nearly faded now. The torch cast weird shadows so the branches of the trees seemed like long fingers, reaching out toward her. She shivered a little, despite the night air not being really cold at this time of year. She did not have a particularly active imagination, but it was easy to believe strange things might happen in these hills.

The faint scent of lavender wafted toward her on the breeze. Strange, she would not have thought lavender would grow on this exposed mountainside. Jack had his nose down, ahead of her now, darting back and fore in the pools of torchlight. "Seek," she encouraged. "Find Huw, where's Huw?" The dog wagged his tail and trotted off again.

"Huw," she called. "Huw, can you hear me?" There was no answer. She shone her torch on the ground and knelt to examine the soft earth for hoof prints. However, like before, it was impossible to tell which might be Seren's hoof marks, and which were the tracks of the mountain ponies.

She trudged on, pausing occasionally to call Huw's name, or to call to Jack. She took it slowly, not wanting to miss her footing in the darkness. She scoured the track for any sign of Huw and his pony, glad to have the dog's company. She drew in a deep breath acknowledging she was otherwise alone. To be sure Glyn and Evan were on the mountain too, but they'd gone in different directions. Here, in the silence, she could almost believe the ghost stories Glyn told her might have some substance. She shivered again trying to concentrate on following Jack and searching for clues which might lead her to the boy.

The track became rougher and stonier the higher she climbed, and she had to be even more careful. The night had drawn in completely now, and although she knew there should be a full moon, it was hardly visible because of the thick cloud cover.

After what felt like several miles, and although she hadn't kept track of the exact distance on her phone, she checked the time. She'd been walking for almost an hour. Nearly time to call Glyn and Evan as arranged, but she hated to give up, and the notion the boy might really be lost chilled her blood. Neither of the men could have found him either, or they would have called her to let her know.

Don't give up now. You're closer than you think.

What? The scent of lavender seemed even stronger and for a fleeting moment Megan fancied she heard a sound like tinkling bells, and someone whispering in her ear. She shivered again. She really was letting her imagination get the better of her. The wind had become stronger now, sending the clouds scudding across the sky, revealing the moon at intervals. When a silver shaft of moonlight filtered through the clouds she studied the track ahead of her. Strewn with several large boulders and a few straggly bushes, it zig-zagged up the mountain. Then a wisp of mist drifted across in front of her and formed into a shape like a young woman in a long, old-fashioned gown, her hair tumbling around her shoulders. Megan passed her hand across her face in disbelief. This had to be a product of her imagination. She must be even more tired than she thought. She put her hand down and stared at the apparition, blinking as the woman pointed somewhere up ahead.

The mist dissipated and the woman disappeared.

The moonlight must have been playing tricks with her mind. She could not help wishing Glyn had never told her the story of Rhiannon and Sion. She shook her head in an effort to clear it and then realised she'd lost sight of Jack. *Oh no, please don't say I've lost Glyn's dog as well.* She sent up a silent prayer *Please, please let me find Huw—and Jack.*

"Jack. *Jack*," she called urgently. "Jack, come back, come back here, boy." Then the sound of his frantic barking sounded from the rise ahead of her. She stumbled over the rough ground as fast as she dared, toward the sound. She rounded a bend to see the dog, tail wagging furiously, hunkered down on his front legs. There, lying under a scraggy-looking gorse bush, was Huw. For a moment she feared he might be unconscious. She almost cried out in relief when his eyes flickered open as she gathered him into her arms. "Huw," she said softly, "Huw, are you all right?"

He smiled up at her. "'Course, I am," he said sleepily.

"What happened, did you fall off your pony?"

"No," he murmured. "I was just tired. I got off to rest. A nice man and a pretty lady found me and stayed with me. They told me to lie quietly, and you'd come and find me."

She dug her phone out of her pocket.

"Glyn—Glyn I've found him. He's all right but very sleepy."

Glyn's sigh of relief was so palpable Megan felt a wave of sympathy sweep over her. After a short pause, he spoke again. "Thank God he's all right, and you, too. Thank you, Megan, thank you. I don't know what I would have done if…I was worried sick—"

"I know, but as I said, he's fine."

"How far up that track are you? Are you far away? I'll come and get you."

"I'm not sure. I don't think we can be more than about a few miles from where we left the SUV but the track's quite rough and it's a bit steep, so be careful. He's so sleepy I don't think it would be fair to ask him to walk. I'd try to carry him myself, but…"

"No, no. He's too heavy for you to carry, and I don't want you risking a fall in the dark. Stay where you are, and I'll find you."

"Okay. I'll stay here with him and Jack."

"I'll just let Evan know. I'll be with you as soon as I can."

"We're not going anywhere." She slipped the phone back into her pocket, then turned her attention back to the boy.

"Your dad will be here in a bit. Don't worry, everything's going to be all right."

Huw nodded, obviously struggling to stay awake but determined to tell her something. "The lady said she was pleased to see Seren again," he murmured. She told me she's Seren's rightful owner, but I can keep her until I'm too big for her." He smiled again, as if at the memory, and closed his eyes once more. After a few moments, he opened his eyes again. "She said the black filly that Ebony had this year is special, and is a gift from her. When the little filly is four years old, she'll take Seren back, and I can have the filly instead." He yawned, obviously struggling to stay awake. "She said to be sure to tell you and Dad what she told me about giving me the new filly," he whispered. "I think she was an angel."

Megan tried to make sense of his words. Who were the two people he'd seen, where were they now? Had he just been dreaming? Or was the 'pretty lady' he'd seen the same ghostly figure she saw a few minutes ago? If so, something strange had happened here on the mountain, and she wasn't sure she believed it.

"The lady said they won't play any more tricks, as long as you and Dad sort yourselves out," Huw added. He gave another huge yawn. "I dunno what she meant by that, do you?"

Megan had a shrewd suspicion, but just shook her head and smiled as he nodded off again.

****

When Glyn's phone rang, breaking through the silence, he breathed a deep sigh, relief flooding through him at Megan's words. "Glyn, I've found him. He's all right, but very sleepy."

He'd despaired of finding Huw himself. The track he'd been following was so steep and narrow, he doubted the boy would have been foolish enough to ride it at night. When he hadn't heard from either Megan or Evan as the hour approached, his heart sank, and he began to imagine the worst.

He was also wracked with guilt, thinking he might have placed Megan in danger. He should have insisted she stay in the car. She didn't know the mountain and he'd had no right to ask her to help him search for the boy. He'd been so frantic with worry when he discovered Huw missing, he hadn't thought it through before calling her number.

To hear her voice now and know both she and Huw were safe was surely an answer to his prayers. Prayers he'd sent up, without any real confidence, as he desperately searched, fearing the worst, and hoping against hope no harm had befallen either of them.

Chapter Twenty

Found

"See, Sion, I knew she would find him...with a bit of help. 'Tis the reason I put a sleeping spell on him, so he would not fret and would stay here instead of riding any further in the dark. I am glad we found him first, so we could keep him safe. I know he has seen us, but I doubt anyone will believe him. They will just think he was dreaming." Invisible once more, Rhiannon drifted closer to Megan and the boy, placing a protective arm around them.

"What about Megan, she saw you, too."

"I think she already suspected we have been living in—" she giggled. *"I suppose I should say 'haunting' her cottage. I think we can trust her, Sion. I had to show myself so she knew she was close to Huw and he was safe. I hoped she would realise I'd been watching over him—and her."*

"And after all the grief you gave me over the pony you told the boy he could have her?"

"Well only until he is too big for her and the filly is old enough for him to ride." She sighed and a soft breeze whispered in the hedgerow. *"I'm sad I will not be able to ride her again for a while. You know how much I love that little horse, but Huw loves her too, and it seems she has taken to him as well. She has never let*

anyone except me ride her before. I know I could have kept her, but it would be cruel to take her away from him."

She turned and Sion placed his arm around her and hugged her to him. "You always were kind-hearted my love. I know what a sacrifice it is, letting her go back to him. I'll need to disenchant her when she returns to you, of course, so she no longer has a solid form." He drew his brows together in a little frown. "I am sorry, Cariad. You would not have had to give her up if I had not played that silly trick on you and put her in Glyn Phillips's field in the first place."

"But she did help to bring him and Megan together again, did she not? Sometimes, Sion, things do happen for a reason."

"Yes, but they are still not really together, are they?"

Rhiannon shrugged a shoulder. "Well, at least they are talking now. We have done all we can, we will just have to wait and see what happens, now."

****

Megan wrapped her arms around the sleeping boy and leant against a large boulder to wait, with Jack stretched out at her feet.

Several times as she waited in the stillness of the night on the mountain, she thought she heard, once again, the tinkling of bells. Occasionally the sweet scent of lavender wafted across, and she could have sworn she sensed someone standing nearby. She didn't get the sense of anything threatening, more like someone standing guard over them. Of course, it must have been her imagination, like the figure she fancied she saw just before she found Huw. The strange dream he'd told her about sounded very much like Rhiannon, though, the ghost Glyn told her haunted her cottage. She shook her head disparagingly. She'd really believe the cottage *was* haunted next. Glyn had told her the story of Rhiannon and Sion Sienco in front of Huw and had probably told him the tale before, since he was so fond of recounting the old Welsh myths. So Huw would know all about Rhiannon's love for her pony, and his subconscious must somehow have woven her and the pony into his dreams. That still didn't explain the ghostly figure she'd seen, however. Had it been it just a drift of mountain mist causing her tired mind to imagine things—or had she really seen the spirit of Rhiannon?

It seemed like waiting an eternity, when in reality it was probably rather less than an hour before she heard the sound of footsteps on the rocky ground. Then Glyn appeared before her, lowering his torch as she blinked up at him, with a little sigh of relief.

"Megan, *cariad*. Megan, how can I ever thank you, or make it up to you?" He knelt and enfolded both her and Huw in his arms. When he drew back, she saw his eyes glistening in the torchlight and realised he had tears in his eyes. She trembled, trying to remain composed, when she felt fairly close to tears herself. Clearly this man loved his son more than anything in the world, and she was desperately fond of the boy herself.

"Jack found him, really," she said. "He was fast asleep under the gorse."

"Did he say anything?"

"Nothing that made much sense. I was afraid he'd fallen off his pony, but he said he just got off her to rest. He seems to have been dreaming about those two ghosts you told me about, Megan and Sion. He said he'd seen 'a pretty lady' and a 'nice man'. He'll probably tell you himself when he's had a good night's sleep." She paused. "You might want to get him checked over by a doctor, tomorrow though, just in case, but I think he's only tired."

"I've let Clarissa know, and I called Evan to tell him you've found Huw and he's all right. I told him to go back to your vehicle," Glyn said. He looked around. "Any sign of his pony?"

Megan shook her head. "No, she wasn't here when I found Huw. I can only think she's wandered off somewhere."

"Damn, I bet she still had her halter on, too. Luckily she wasn't saddled. I checked the tack room, and it was still locked. He hadn't taken her saddle or bridle, just her halter. Let's hope she doesn't get a foot caught in the halter rope." He gave a regretful shrug of his shoulders. "Unfortunately, there's nothing we can do about it now. I'll have to come back tomorrow and look for her and make sure she's all right."

Glyn glanced down at the sleeping boy and, rising to his feet, took him in his arms. "He's out for the count." He looked at her, his eyes filled with anxiety. "He *is* all right, isn't he? He wasn't delirious or anything when you found him?"

"No," she assured him, "just tired, as I said. He mumbled something about seeing two people, a young man and woman, like I told you, but I think he just fell asleep up here and was dreaming."

The journey back to the vehicle seemed shorter than when Megan had climbed along the track in search of Huw. Then she'd been careful, trying to spot hoof prints, and not lose her way, or trip in the moonlight, and the downhill trip was easier with Glyn to guide her. Evan waited for them by the SUV, as instructed and seemed as relieved to see Huw safe and well as Glyn had been.

She drove with Evan in the front passenger seat and Glyn sitting in the back, cradling Huw who still slept. Jack had leapt into the back of the vehicle as well, and lay curled up by Glyn's feet.

"I'll run you home first, shall I?" she said to Evan. "Then I can take Glyn and Huw back to their place on my way back to my cottage." She knew Evan lived somewhere near the village, and it was easy enough to turn around and head for Pentrebont, when they hit the lane once more.

"Thanks," he said. "If you're sure it's not too much trouble, like."

"Of course not. It's been an eventful night, and I'm sure you wouldn't want to have to walk the rest of the way home. Just tell me how far your house is, and I'll drop you off." She shot a quick glance over her shoulder. "That all right with you, Glyn?"

"It's very good of you," he replied. "I really don't know what we'd have done without you, with both our vehicles off the road. I'll phone the garage tomorrow, Evan, and arrange for someone to fix my pick-up and sort out your van."

"Thanks. I dunno how I forgot the spare wheel. I'm usually so careful about things like that."

"Well, these things happen. It's just unfortunate my pick-up should be out of action, too. If it wasn't for Megan here, I don't know what we'd have done."

"Well, I'm just glad I came back in time," she said,

feeling her cheeks grow pink and glad neither man could see her in the dark.

"Thanks, Megan," Evan said, when she pulled up outside his little cottage. "My wife's got supper keeping hot on the stove for me if I'm lucky. I called her earlier to tell her what was happening, so hopefully I won't get an ear bashin'. Goodnight."

"'Night, Evan," she said, as he closed the door and walked up the cobblestone drive.

"Goodnight, and thanks again," Glyn called out after him.

"You and Huw all right staying in the back?" Megan asked, with another glance over her shoulder.

"Yes, we're fine. No point waking Huw now, just to get in the front seat."

They drove in silence back to Hafod Farm. Megan stopped the SUV in the stable yard and came round to hold open the door, so Glyn could lift Huw from the car without waking him."

"Thanks. You'll come up to the house with us? Have a cup of tea and something to eat? It's the least I can do after me dragging you out so late and you finding Huw—"

Megan shook her head. "No, I'd better be getting back. It is late, like you said, and you'll be wanting to get Huw to bed."

"Please. We need to talk."

"What about your wife?"

"I called her to tell her we found Huw, as soon as you let me know. She was very relieved of course. I told her you were the one who found him."

She caught her breath and her heart seemed to skip a beat. That wasn't quite what she'd meant. She had so many questions to ask, but now was not the time.

"Please," Glyn repeated. "I need to explain—"

"Tomorrow. I'll come over tomorrow. You need to take care of Huw tonight. I'm on leave so I don't need to go into work for a few days."

She wasn't in the mood for a confrontation with Clarissa just now. Presumably she was in the house waiting for Glyn's arrival with the boy. Giving him no chance to argue further, she leapt back into the driver's seat and drove away as fast as she could, her mind racing.

****

For the second time in two days, Glyn watched Megan drive away, and his heart sank. He had so much to be grateful to her for, so much he needed to tell her. Perhaps she was right though, the hour was late, and it might be easier to explain things to her in the morning.

The sleeping boy stirred in his arms. He needed to get him safely tucked up in his own bed. As he held him closer, his eyes flickered open.

"Dad?"

"Yes, son, you're safe now, but what were you thinking? Do you know how worried I've been?"

"Dad, please don't send me away, don't make me leave you."

"Don't be silly," Glyn whispered. "Of course I won't send you away. No one's going to make you go anywhere. Whatever put that idea in your head?"

Chapter Twenty-One

Reconciliation and Confrontation

"Perhaps we should not make a habit of sneakin' into these automobiles, Rhiannon, my love."

"Phsssht, I quite like it. It makes a change from drifting around in the air like a bit of mist. Anyway, I wish to keep an eye on Megan, she is not in the best frame of mind, and I want to make sure she gets home safely."

"You watch over everyone. It is what I love about you."

Rhiannon laid a gentle hand on his arm. "Not everyone. Only those I have a special interest in. Anyway, since I might aspire to be a guardian angel I have to act like one, do I not?"

****

Try as she might to keep her mind clear as she drove back to the cottage, myriad thoughts whirled through Megan's mind, however hard she attempted to blank them out.

She parked the car, and once indoors, switched on the light and set the kettle to boil. She most definitely needed a cup of tea. Her limbs felt heavy, and her head ached with weariness and exhaustion. She almost wished she had accepted Glyn's offer. She wasn't sure she had the strength to listen to what he wanted to tell her just then, though, especially if Clarissa was there too. It had been an eventful night and all she wanted to do now was sleep.

She made a cup of tea and went to the cupboard where she kept her favourite double choc-chip cookies. There might be one or two left. She'd meant to replenish her stock last time she shopped in the village, but somehow it had slipped her mind. To her surprise, the tin contained a fresh new packet. She shook her head in confusion. How could she suddenly be so absent minded? Perhaps the ghosts were playing tricks on her—or perhaps she was just overtired.

She relaxed a little and mulled over the evening's events. Thank goodness Huw had not come to any harm. Glyn had sounded frantic when he called her. She could only imagine how grief-stricken he would have been if anything happened to the boy. And what about Clarissa?

She tried to make some sense of the confusion in her mind. From what Clarissa had said the previous day, it seemed Glyn and his estranged wife were planning a reconciliation. Then he'd called her *cariad* when he got to her and Huw on the mountain. *Cariad*, a term of endearment and a word he used sparingly as if it meant something. She sighed. The moment had been an emotional one, and he'd probably been so relieved he didn't think about what he was saying. She still didn't want to believe he'd been deceiving her those past weeks, but what else was she supposed to think?

And that story of Huw's—what an imagination the boy had. She hoped Glyn would be able to find the pony in the morning. Huw was so fond of her and the little mare had certainly given him a lot of self-confidence. Well, no doubt Glyn would track her down. She might have joined one of the small herds running semi-wild, and although she'd probably give him a run for his money, Megan had faith Glyn would catch up with her in the end.

She sighed and rinsed her cup and plate before running the shower. She would have loved to indulge in a long soak in the bath, but her eyes would hardly stay open, and she didn't want to go to sleep in the bathtub. After showering, she crawled into bed and switched out the light, then snuggled under the bedclothes. The scent of lavender wafted through the open window. Her mind wandered off and brought her dreams of an ethereal woman made of moonlight, and wearing a long flowing robe, with a girdle of little bells. She rode a pony with gossamer wings, which suddenly unfurled from the smooth, chestnut coat as it flew into the night sky.

She woke when her alarm went off and cursed under her breath. She'd intended to sleep in, that morning, but had forgotten to alter the alarm on her phone. She lay there for a while, going over the events of the previous evening. Then she dressed and prepared a breakfast of yoghurt and fresh raspberries, followed by some wholemeal toast and honey. She lingered over breakfast, putting off her visit to Hafod Farm. She'd said she would go there to talk with Glyn, but now she wondered if she'd made the right decision. Part of her longed to see him again, and while it would most likely be painful, she needed to hear his explanation of his relationship with Clarissa. While she really didn't relish the idea of confronting the woman, she had things she wanted to say to her, too.

On second thoughts though, would it be better not

to go? Emotions had been running high last night. Glyn had been grateful to her for finding Huw, but in the cold light of morning he might regret having agreed to see her today.

No sooner had the thought entered her head than her mobile rang. She checked the caller—Glyn. She took a deep breath before she answered.

"Megan—I just wanted to check that you're okay."

"I'm fine, why wouldn't I be?" The words came out more sharply than she'd intended but she was still not sure how she should react. His voice sounded concerned, but for all she knew he could have Clarissa beside him, breathing down his neck.

"I was just a bit worried after last night, it was something of an eventful evening."

"Yes. How's Huw?"

"He's asleep again, although he did wake for a short while, earlier. I called the doctor first thing this morning, to check him over. He said he's fine, and there's no sign of concussion, or any evidence he hit his head. I said I'd let him have a lie-in after last night's excitement. Good job there are still a few days of the school holidays left."

"Thank goodness," she said. "I'm so glad he's okay."

"Oh, and Seren came back. Strangest thing, when I got up this morning she was back in the paddock, as if she'd been there all the time." The line went quiet for a few moments before he went on, "You will come over this morning, won't you?"

She hesitated for a moment, then came to a decision. Despite his gratitude for last night, she felt sure he wanted to break up with her, face to face—and she supposed Clarissa would be there to gloat. Part of her hoped she would be, so she could tell the other woman what she thought of her. The other part hoped she'd have the decency to keep out of the way while he broke it to her that he and Clarissa were getting back together—if such was his intention. She did not relish going to Ty Gwyn, but Glyn owed her an explanation, and the longer they delayed talking, the harder it would be.

"All right. What time would you like me to come over?"

"Whenever you're ready, I won't be going anywhere until I've spoken to you."

"Okay, give me an hour and I'll be there." She ended the call and sipped her tea, trying to compose herself for what she feared might be the worst day of her life.

****

Glyn strode across the yard as soon as he spotted Megan's SUV approaching the gate into the yard. He swung it open for her and watched while she parked. When she stepped out of the vehicle, he stepped close to her and took both her hands in his.

"Megan, you have no idea how much I've missed you. Let's go up to the house. As I said, we need to talk." He dropped her hands and put his arm lightly about her shoulders. She took a deep breath, and he felt her tremble. He did not remove his arm from her shoulders. She looked so vulnerable, and he was relieved she made no effort to shrug his arm away. Once inside the house, he motioned to her to sit on the settee by the window in the living room. The two dogs immediately came over to lie at her feet.

"Would you like a drink, or something to eat? Have you had breakfast?"

"Yes, I ate before I came, I'm fine, thanks." She gazed around as if looking for something—or someone, and he seated himself beside her, taking her hand in his.

"Megan, I know Clarissa turning up like she did was a shock. I'm so sorry. I should have sent her packing straight away, but I was as stunned by her arrival as you were. I was beside myself when you didn't answer my calls, and when you messaged me to say you were going away and I passed your cottage yesterday, and saw your car was missing..." He tried not to let his voice betray the pain he felt. "I had a feeling I might never see you again."

"I was only gone for best part of the day. I just had to get away. I-I didn't want to complicate things if you and Clarissa were getting back together again, and I just needed time to come to terms with it, and to try to figure out what to do next."

He winced inwardly and squeezed her hand. "And did you?"

She gave him a questioning look, tilting her head to one side, almost as if her mind had wandered onto something else. "Did I what?"

"Figure out what you wanted to do next?"

She gave a wan smile. "No, not really. I just kept imagining you and Clarissa together and I felt so miserable I couldn't really make any proper decisions. I'd intended to have a few days away but in the end, I decided to come back—just as well, as it happens."

Glyn sighed, cursing himself for hurting her so much, and put his arm around her, drawing her close. "Oh Megan, Clarissa and I were never going to get together again. Her coming to see me was completely out of the blue. I had no idea she intended turning up like that, and I certainly don't want a reconciliation."

She gazed at him as if she couldn't believe what she heard. "Then—then she's not going to be moving back in with you permanently?"

"No way. What on earth gave you *that* idea, cariad?"

For a moment she didn't answer, then she said, "Clarissa came to see me, the day after she arrived. She brought back an old sweater I must have left here. She made it sound like you were a couple again. She…she warned me off."

"She—what?" He tried not to show his anger, in case Megan thought it was directed at her. "What in Heaven's name did Clarissa think she was doing? She had no right to do that. I'm so sorry if she gave you the impression we were getting back together, sweetheart. I'd already told her it was never going to happen, although it sounds like she's convinced herself I'll change my mind." He took a deep breath. "Our divorce can't come through quickly enough for me. This is the first time she's even been here, and to be honest I thought she was out of my life. I never expected to see her again. And before you ask, she's been staying at the Red Dragon, in Aberystwyth. She didn't want to stay in Pentrebont apparently, and anyway the local hotels and guest houses are full at this time of year."

"You mean…? I wondered where she was. I thought she'd be staying here."

He shook his head and drew her even closer. "No, I wasn't going to jeopardise the divorce, with it being so close to finalising, by allowing her to sleep under the same roof as myself. No wonder you didn't want to speak to me. You must have believed I'd been lying about how I felt about you, all the time."

She nodded mutely, and he could see the relief as well as questions in her eyes.

"I'm sorry Glyn, I should have trusted you and answered your messages…given you chance to explain. It's just—Clarissa made it seem…she told me you were getting back together again. She made it seem like a *fait accompli*."

Glyn kissed the top of her head and sighed. "She never did like taking 'no' for an answer. She's used to getting her own way, but I can't believe she'd have told you we were getting back together." He frowned. "It sounds like she was trying to get you out of the way so she could try and manipulate me into giving in."

"So that *is* what she came here for?"

"Apparently—well that's what she said she wanted, at first. She came here yesterday afternoon and tried to get me to change my mind. I thought I'd made it clear there was no chance of that. Then she said she would try to get sole custody of Huw, or at least parental rights to have him stay with her in France, more or less permanently." He set his mouth in a hard line. "I'd like to see her try, and I can't help wondering if she has a hidden agenda."

"What? How could she suddenly come back like that and demand sole custody?"

"It seems she and her boyfriend have split up," he told her, trying to keep the bitterness out of his voice. "At first, she made out she regretted leaving us and wanted us to be together again, as a family. Then, when I stressed there was no possibility of that happening, she tried to persuade Huw to go with her when she goes back to France." He paused and put out a hand to absently fondle Bob who nuzzled his leg for attention.

"How…how did Huw feel about that?" Megan asked, her voice husky.

Glyn sighed. "I told him he was free to choose if he wanted to go or not. As soon as Clarissa left yesterday, I sat him down and did my best to explain the situation to him, and again made it clear if he wanted to go to France with his mother I would not stand in his way. He didn't say much at the time, but I had the distinct feeling he wasn't keen on the idea. It's a terrible thing to say, but his mother is a complete stranger to him. She hasn't even so much as sent him a birthday or Christmas card since she left us."

"Then why? Why does she suddenly want him now?"

Again he shook his head. "Who knows? Guilt perhaps, or maybe she feels he's now at an age she can cope with. She was never very maternal, even when he was a baby, and when he was a toddler it was always left to me to do most of the caring for him. Not that I minded, he was, and always will be my pride and joy. The thing is, after she left me, it was something of a relief. We'd been growing further and further apart and fighting over the least little thing. That's not the sort of environment I wanted Huw to grow up in."

She gave him a little sympathetic smile. "I can understand that."

He took her hand again and kissed her palm, giving it another little squeeze. "I've kept myself pretty much to myself since I moved here, and people will always speculate. I've heard the rumours about my wife having died or been killed in a tragic accident. I've said nothing to dispel—or confirm—them. I suppose it's cowardly of me, but I found it easier to let people think my wife had died, rather than having deserted me and our son. I'd told Huw she had to go away but she still loved him, and I would always be here to care for him." He paused for a moment before continuing. "I thought she'd finally accepted the divorce was going to go through. However, since her breakup with the man she left me for, she appears to have decided it was worth a last-ditch attempt to stop it. She still seems to have some demented idea I'll change my mind—which I won't."

Talking about this was not easy, but he owed it to Megan to tell her everything. "I want you to know, I've never tried to stop her having access to Huw all the time she's been away. Nor did I keep her a secret from Huw or try to turn him against her. Whatever her faults, she's still his mother. Huw might be the only decent thing—the only really good thing—to come from our marriage, but I wouldn't deny her the right to see her own child, if she wanted it."

Megan bit her lip, a very tender look in her eyes. "I can't imagine how any woman, especially his own mother, wouldn't want to care for—and love—a boy like Huw."

"Neither can I, but it seems he wasn't very high on her list of priorities—until now, anyway." He sighed again. "You know, I have so much to thank you for. Huw's very lucky you found him last night. When I think what could have happened…" A thought occurred to him. "You said he was asleep when you found him. He must have had some very vivid dreams. He told me he'd seen 'a lady' and she said she owned the pony, and he could keep her until he outgrew her."

Megan nodded. "I know. He told me the same thing. He also said the little black filly that was foaled late, was a gift from her. He said she told him to tell you he should have it for his own, and she would take Seren back when he grows too big for her." She gave a little half smile. "I don't think it was something he made up to get you to give him the filly. I think he really believed what he said."

She hesitated, as if not sure if she should say what was on her mind, or whether to keep it to herself. Finally, she looked at him with a wry smile. "Glyn, do you think there *are* such things as ghosts, or am I going a little crazy? I could have sworn I saw the ghostly figure of a woman beckoning me near to where I found Huw, and then she just disappeared."

He shook his head. "I don't know *cariad*. The imagination can play funny tricks on a person, especially at night on the mountain. I already had it in mind to raise the filly for Huw. By the time she's big enough to ride, Huw will have outgrown Seren, the way he's shooting up. I'm not sure why, but it seemed quite logical when I first had the idea, almost as if the foal was born for that very reason." He chuckled. "Perhaps we're both a little mad, or perhaps I've been telling you too many legends and ghost stories."

"Or perhaps they really do exist after all?" she said with a quizzical expression in her eyes.

Before he could reply, both dogs stood, and Jack gave a long, low bark.Glyn let Megan go and turned to the window to see a car turning into the drive. A car he now knew only too well—Clarissa.

Chapter Twenty-Two

The Agreement

Rhiannon's misty form, invisible to Megan and Glyn, shimmered in annoyance. "Now what, Sion? Just as I thought these two were about to get back together again, this woman has to come back. I think I might just materialise and frighten the life out of her, perhaps she will leave Glyn alone then."

"Now, now Rhiannon," Sion soothed. "Don't you go doin' anything so rash. Glyn is quite capable of handlin' her without our help. Let us just sit here in the shadows an' see what happens."

"Well, all right then. But if she gets too high-handed, I am going to scare her so much she will never set foot in this part of Wales ever again, that I am."

****

Glyn turned from the window and gave Megan a brief hug. "It's Clarissa. Damn! I thought we'd said all we had to say to each other. Are you up to seeing her, or shall I tell her to go away?"

Megan had already prepared herself for a confrontation. Much as she hated the thought of seeing Clarissa, she wasn't going to back out now.

"No, it's all right. We're in this together now, Glyn—unless you want to speak to her alone, of course."

"As you said, sweetheart, we're in this together, so long as you're happy with it."

Megan drew in a deep breath. If Clarissa intended to have a go at her for being there, when the other woman had specifically told her to keep away, she'd be in for a shock. Megan wasn't going to let her demoralize her this time. She'd give Clarissa as good as she got.

As soon as Glyn opened the door, Clarissa swept in and strode into the living room. She stopped in front of the painting of Huw riding Seren, which hung in pride of place on the wall above the fireplace.

"Nice painting, I didn't really notice it when I was here before. Did you have someone from London come down to paint it?"

"No," Glyn replied from behind her. "As a matter of fact, Megan painted it. It's rather good, don't you think." Clarissa muttered something Megan didn't catch, and sat down, uninvited, in the comfortable easy chair opposite where she sat. The woman gave a slight start when she first spotted Megan, although she didn't acknowledge her. Obviously shocked to see her there, she shot her a glare. Megan held her gaze, determined not to be intimidated. Having fully expected her to be here when she first arrived, she had already steeled herself for a showdown.

Jack jumped up, wagging his tail, and Clarissa frowned and swatted him off with an impatient hand. "Get down dog," she said, and flicked imaginary hairs from her designer jacket, wafting the scent of expensive perfume in Megan's direction.

"Lie down, Jack, good boy," Glyn commanded, bending down to stroke him, and the young dog curled

The Matchmaker's Mare

up obediently by his feet.

"Do you want a coffee?" Glyn asked, ever polite, although Megan noticed he didn't smile.

"No thanks, I won't be staying here too long, seeing you have company." She glowered at Megan as if she'd grown a set of horns. Her expression said as clearly as words *What the hell are you doing here when I warned you off?*

Turning back to Glyn she said, "Although I don't suppose you have anything a bit stronger, like a gin and tonic?"

Glyn shook his head "No, I'm afraid I don't. Anyway, it's a bit early, and you don't really want to be drinking and driving, do you?"

Her pale blue eyes flashed with annoyance and a scowl passed across her perfect features.

"Well, I'm sure one little G and T wouldn't matter. Anyway, I've only come to find out how Huw is. As I said, I won't be staying long."

"He's fine. He didn't come to any harm at all." He nodded in Megan's direction, "Thanks to Megan. He's asleep at the moment."

Clarissa gave her a grudging half smile, which looked anything but genuine. "I suppose I should say 'thanks'."

"No need. I'm only glad I was able to help. I'd have wanted to help search for any youngster alone on the mountain after dark."

Clarissa tossed her head and glared at Glyn. "Anyway, what the devil was he doing riding a pony at that time of night? I'd have thought you'd have more sense than—"

"I didn't know he was out on the mare," Glyn told

her, his tone slow and patient, as if he was keeping control of his temper with an effort. "I'd tucked him up in bed earlier last evening, and thought he was fast asleep. I was busy sorting out some paperwork and accounts when Evan came to tell me he'd seen him riding off and—well you know the rest. I let you know he'd gone missing before we set off to search for him, and I notice you didn't bother to come yourself."

A slight flush spread across her face. "Hmm, well there wasn't very much I could do was there? I didn't have any shoes suitable for scrambling up mountains and it would have taken at least twenty minutes to drive here from Aberystwyth." She stared at a painted fingernail for a moment. "I did stay on the line in case I was needed, I was really worried you know, and very relieved when you let me know he'd been found. I still can't imagine what he was doing riding in these mountains when he should have been asleep."

Glyn remained silent for a few moments. Then he stood and went over to a small side-table and picked up a scrap of paper. "I found this note on his bed after he went missing." With a grim expression, he handed it to her. She gave a little sigh of exasperation before reading the words written on it, then let it slip from her fingers onto the carpet, where Glyn retrieved it.

All the blood drained from her face. "I-I don't understand. He says he's running away because he doesn't want me to take him away to France with me?"

Megan glanced at Clarissa. The woman seemed genuinely shaken. Perhaps she did care about her son, despite everything.

"So, it would seem," Glyn said. "I couldn't get much out of him after we found him last night, but when we got him home, he begged me not to send him away. I have to take responsibility and say it was my fault. I obviously hadn't explained it to him very well. He seemed to be under the impression that I actually *wanted* him to go with you because I'd told him I wouldn't stop him going with you if that's what he wanted. I had quite a time trying to convince him he didn't have to go anywhere he didn't want to." He paused and rubbed the edge of his chin. "I'm not absolutely sure I got through to him, even then, he was still half asleep."

Megan almost felt sorry for Clarissa. She looked completely deflated and slumped back onto the cushions, her usually smooth brow creased in a frown. When she replied her voice shook a little, losing its sharp edge. "I-I had no idea he felt so strongly. Of course I wouldn't have tried to force him to leave here. I thought he'd have been excited to go to France with me. I don't suppose he's ever been through the channel tunnel, has he?"

****

Glyn had some difficulty in keeping his tone even and not raising it in annoyance. "He hasn't seen you since he was two and a half years old, Clarissa. You've had no contact with him for over six years. You can't expect him to be happy at the prospect of leaving everything he knows, his home, school, friends—me—to go to France with someone who's a virtual stranger."

Clarissa examined her perfectly manicured nails again for a moment. "Well, I suppose when you put it like that…" After a long, awkward pause, she set her lips in a firm line and looked at Glyn. She pointedly ignored Megan, who looked as if she was keen to say something and trying hard to keep quiet

"I assume you're still determined to go through with this divorce?"

He sighed, his patience beginning to run short. "We've already been through this. I haven't changed my mind overnight! It's a bit late to go back on it now, since the *Final Order*'s already applied for and I'm expecting it to go through any day." He paused, a frown darkening his brow, before continuing, "You know how much I hate the idea of divorce. I've always believed in the sanctity of marriage, but you have to admit after six years there's little point in remaining in a relationship which is, to all intents and purposes, dead in the water. Neither of us would be happy, and I hate to think what it would do to Huw."

Clarissa scowled. "I suppose *she* has nothing to do with it?" she said, her hostile gaze now directed at Megan. "You looked pretty chummy when the three of you rode into the yard together the day I arrived."

Glyn glanced across at Megan. She looked pale but had a determined tilt to her chin. She was such a contrast to Clarissa, whose bleached, elaborately styled hair and skilfully applied make-up couldn't hold a candle to Megan's fresh, natural beauty.

He wondered what he'd ever seen in Clarissa. He did not normally have a problem keeping his temper under control, but he wasn't going to allow her to involve Megan in their quarrel. "It has nothing to do with Megan. You gave me sufficient grounds for divorce on desertion alone, not to mention you went off with someone else. Six years, Clarissa. Six years, when you didn't even keep in touch."

Clarissa had the grace to look uncomfortable but

did not drop her defiant attitude.

"I had things going on. I've been busy, after buying a small property and starting a fashion business in France. Then James and I separated, and I've only just been able to find the time to come back here and track you down in this god-forsaken place. Her tone changed to one of wheedling. "I know I've made mistakes, but I did think perhaps you and I…"

For a moment Glyn could hardly believe she would bring that up again. "You have the temerity to say that now—after leaving me for another man?" He gritted his teeth, leaning forward and trying to keep his temper in check. "I waited five years before filing for divorce, when I didn't have to, and you had plenty of chance to try and mend our marriage if you'd really wanted to."

"I just admitted I made a mistake, didn't I? As I told you, James and I are not together anymore, anyway."

"Well, I'm afraid it's much too late to talk about reconciliation now, Clarissa, as I've already told you several times, and I meant it. I've moved on with my life, and as far as I'm concerned, the sooner our divorce is finalised, the better. You killed everything I once felt for you the day you left me and our small son, to be with him."

"Yes, well it's certainly obvious you've *moved on*," she said, twisting her lips in a sneer, giving Megan another pointed look.

"Don't bring me into this," Megan stated, before Glyn had the chance to tell Clarissa to leave her out of it.

"Why not? I suppose you're very pleased with yourself, stealing both my husband and my son."

"I haven't *stolen* either of them as you put it," Megan told her, rising to her feet, and a wave of pride rose up in him. She looked so fierce and determined. He'd not expected her to confront Clarissa, but she seemed well able to stand up for herself.

"I'm quite sure Glyn would have done everything he could to save your marriage if he believed it worth saving," she went on. "As for Huw, I've no intention of trying to take your place as his birth mother, but if he wants me to, I'll do my damnedest to give him all the love and affection he's been missing from you. How can you call yourself a mother when you left him as a small child?" She remained standing for several more moments, and Glyn glanced at Clarissa who'd gone very pale. He had never seen her lose her composure or look quite so uneasy. Megan gave her a hard look, as if restraining herself from saying more, before seating herself once more by his side.

"It seems there's no point in arguing with either of you then," Clarissa said in a voice devoid of emotion. "You've obviously decided to cut me out of Huw's life and there doesn't seem much I can do about it, until I see my solicitor, that is." She paused, as if for effect. "I intend to file for custody," she said slowly. "Judges tend to prefer to give custody to the mother."

Glyn almost laughed at her audacity. "You're welcome to try," he said. "First of all, I would never cut you out of Huw's life, but if it goes to a family court, I really can't see any judge granting you custody. For a start, I've been both mother and father to him for six years, and he's made it quite clear he wants to stay here, with me. I think last night's escapade confirms that. Since you deserted him when he was a toddler and have had no contact with him until now—"

"All right, all right." she interrupted, with a sniff. "I suppose it would probably be a long, drawn-out process if I *were* to go for custody and I don't *really* need the hassle at the moment. However, I could still make things very difficult for you …"

Glyn took a deep breath and drummed his fingers on the coffee table in front of him. He had a shrewd idea what all this was leading up to. "Very well, Clarissa. In the end, surely, we both want what's best for Huw. Enough with the threats and beating about the bush. Yes, you could make things difficult, not to mention expensive, and drag out the inevitable. As far as the divorce is concerned, since you've been served with the petition, on the grounds of over five years separation there's not much you can do about it. I'd prefer to keep things as amicable as possible, but don't forget I *could* also have cited adultery on your part." He let his words sink in before he went on, "We both know it's highly unlikely you would get a custody order under the circumstances, but I really don't want to put Huw through the trauma of a court battle. I don't believe you're talking about wanting to get back with me because of any lingering affection you might harbour for me, either. So, let's get down to what you really want shall we? How much is it going to take for you to just go away and agree to me having full custody?"

A sardonic smile played about her lips. "As we've already established, I *do* have a business in France, and I intend to stay there. Is that far enough away for you?" Without giving him chance to reply, she went on, "And all right, I'll admit it—I have a few debts…"

Now they were getting to it. "How much?" he demanded, with a cold edge to his voice.

"Forty thousand, and I want visiting rights." For just a moment she looked a little unsure of herself. "If Huw wants to, of course. I won't force him into anything."

Glyn did his best to keep his expression impassive as he noticed Megan draw in a sharp breath. At last! He was sure this was what Clarissa had been after all along. He made some mental calculations and considered what he was going to have to give up. The equestrian business, although doing well for him at the moment, could be unpredictable. He wanted to make sure he had enough to fall back on if the business should fall on hard times, and to provide for Huw should anything ever happen to himself.

After his conversation with Megan, he'd decided to pursue his dream of starting a riding school, since he could now afford to hire an assistant instructor to spread the load. His plan had been to build some more looseboxes, adjoining the existing stable block, and to purchase some quiet riding school ponies as well as new saddlery and other equipment.

He checked some figures on his phone. What she was asking would make a hefty dent in his savings and then some. He would have to put his dream on hold, and make sure he still had a bit of a buffer for emergencies, not counting the sum he'd put in trust for Huw. At the moment, the happiness and peace of mind of his son mattered more than money in the bank or his own ambitions.

"I'll give you your forty thousand, as a final and complete settlement, but I want your written promise you won't try to contest custody. You can visit by arrangement, write to Huw, and contact him by email if you want to. When he's older, if he wishes to, he can visit you in France, but it has to be his choice."

She hesitated for a few moments, and he could not quite decide if this was because she was considering his offer, or wondering if she could have asked for more and got away with it.

"All right," she said at last. "I accept."

"And I have your word on that?"

Another long pause. "Yes…you do."

"I'll transfer half the money into your account immediately. I'll need your bank details."

After she got out her smartphone and read out the account numbers to him, he made the necessary transaction. He let her confirm the amount and details and hit *Transfer*.

"I'll see my solicitor tomorrow to draw up an Agreement both on the financial settlement and clean break order, and the custody issue," he said. "I'll let you know when the documents are ready for your signature."

"What about the rest of my settlement?"

"You'll get that as soon as you've signed the agreement."

When she remained silent, he continued, "I'm really *not* trying to cut you out of his life, Clarissa. You are his mother, but I don't want him traumatised by us fighting it out in court, if it can be avoided."

"I understand," she said, rising to her feet. "Whatever you may think of me, and despite the fact I may have been somewhat neglectful of my duty as a mother, I do still care about the boy. You know where

I'm staying. I'll expect to hear from you as soon as the documents are ready to sign."

He nodded wordlessly. There didn't seem to be anything else to say.

"Could I see him before I leave?" she asked, standing, and half turning toward the stairs.

"I'd really prefer not to wake him just yet," he told her. "I'll have a chat with him and explain you're going back to France and would like to see him tomorrow, just to say goodbye."

"As you wish. I'll see you tomorrow then."

Without another word, she strode to the door. Glyn showed her out and heaved a sigh of relief as he watched her walk into the yard and drive off in her flashy sports car, vaguely aware of Megan standing just behind him. He wasn't sure how badly Clarissa needed his money. She certainly showed every sign of not being short of cash. But then she'd also said she had debts. Perhaps her show of affluence was a front, and she'd overstretched herself financially and needed to pay back loans on things like that expensive car.

Whatever the truth, it would be worth every penny to know he wouldn't have to see the pain and confusion in his son's eyes again.

Chapter Twenty-Three

Aftermath

"Well, thank goodness she has gone at last. I thought I was going to have to use my powers of persuasion on Glyn, but he managed it all by himself."

"I think he has more intuition than you gave him credit for, Rhiannon my sweet." Sion gave his wife a soft kiss on the cheek.

"Yes, well I am pleased he sent her packing."

"I will admit, for a moment there, I did wonder if she might wheedle her way back into his affections."

Rhiannon smiled and gave him a gentle nudge. *"Not, a chance, Sion. He is not so silly. He loves Megan, and he will be so much better off with her, rather than that selfish, self-centred hussy."*

"Well for once I can't argue with you, cariad, much as I'd like to."

Megan and Glyn were too engrossed in each other to notice a small cushion fly across the back of the room. Nor did they hear the soft chuckle which could have been mistaken for the breeze whispering in the trees.

****

Whether from relief that Clarissa had gone or just the emotion of the moment, Megan could not be sure, but Glyn turned and took her in his arms. He kissed her with such tenderness she almost sobbed. She trembled and pressed closer to him. He deepened the kiss, and his tongue teased hers, his kiss becoming fiercer and more urgent. His arms tightened around her, making her oblivious to everything except her need for him. She could no longer hide her love, or pretend he was no more than a friend. He'd kept his promise to take things slow ever since that first kiss, and this was the first really passionate embrace they'd ever shared, but it felt so right.

At last, he slowly ended their kiss and released her.

"I'm so sorry you had to be involved in this," he said. "I should have guessed she might turn up today, but I wouldn't have asked you over if I'd known—"

She squeezed his arm. "Don't worry," she told him. "I was prepared for a confrontation. Don't forget, I thought she'd been staying here, so I'd hyped myself up for you to tell me you were getting back together."

"As if that was likely to happen—but of course you didn't know at the time, did you? I wish I'd realised Clarissa was going to confront you like she did, before you went away. I'd have stopped her somehow."

"She made a point of telling me you didn't know she intended coming to see me. She, more or less, accused me of trying to take you and Huw away from her then, too. The way she spoke I was convinced you and she were getting back together. Don't worry," she said, as he wrinkled his forehead in concern, "I told her a few home truths before she left in a huff."

Glyn's expression lightened then, but he shook his head disparagingly. "I'm beginning to wish I *had* woken Huw, so she could say goodbye to him now, so she needn't come back tomorrow. I really want to talk

The Matchmaker's Mare

to him first though. I want to make sure he understands that while I'll support him if he wants to see her in France when he's older, no one will force him to do so."

Megan took his hand. "I think you did the right thing," she said. "He might have been really upset if he saw her before you'd had chance to talk to him about it."

He drew in his breath. "I'm really not looking forward to speaking to her again. The sooner she's out of our lives the better."

"That was quite a hefty sum she demanded wasn't it!" She stopped and felt her cheeks flush. "Sorry, I didn't mean to pry…I mean it's not really any of my business."

"It's all right," he said, squeezing her hand, "and it is your business too, if we're to have any future together. You're right. It's a lot of money, but don't worry, I can sell off a few spare acres of land, and I've made sure there'll be a little in reserve for emergencies." He paused for a moment, before going on. "The small farm I had in south Wales went for a good price, enough for me to purchase this place without having to take out much of a mortgage, so I can easily increase it if necessary. Hafod was quite run down when I bought it, so I got it for a reasonable price. It needed a lot of renovation work to the outbuildings and fencing—"

She gave him a questioning look.

"But it looks so well maintained and cared for."

He smiled. "Thanks. I was able to do a lot of it myself and improve the place gradually, with some help from Evan and his family, so it didn't eat into my reserves too much. I've managed to put a fair bit away from my pony sales and training fees, as well, so I can manage to pay off Clarissa without going over my head in debt. It may mean delaying one or two of my plans though, but they can wait."

She gave a little sigh. "It just seems wrong you had to buy her co-operation like that." He had a rather wistful expression in his eyes. Megan had the feeling there was something he didn't want to go into, about those plans. She wouldn't press him just now, but she hoped he would confide in her when he was ready.

"I think she knew deep down she had no real chance of fighting me either for the divorce or for custody, after being away for so long," Glyn told her, still holding her hand. "I have a feeling it was the money she wanted all along. She could certainly have made the whole process take much longer, if she'd decided to be difficult or fight me for custody. In the end it was worth the money to have her promise to sign the agreement."

He drew her close again. "I can't forget the expression on your face the night she arrived unannounced, waiting for us when we came back from our ride."

She chewed her bottom lip. "I was devastated when she said she was your wife. She made it sound like I had no right to be anywhere near you."

"I'll never forgive myself for not setting her straight immediately. I was so shaken by her sudden appearance—but that's no excuse for my weakness. I should have made it perfectly clear that I wanted nothing more to do with her and I was with you now."

Her voice trembled "We'd…we'd had such a

wonderful day, and then, when I saw her in the yard, I overreacted. I—I really thought she'd come back to you, and it was what you wanted. The more I thought about it, the more I convinced myself you must have been lying to me about not caring for her anymore."

****

Her words cut into his heart like a knife. No wonder she hadn't returned his calls.

"Sweetheart, I stopped caring for her a long time ago. Our marriage was a terrible mistake. We married without really knowing each other, and I realise now our feelings were based more on infatuation than real affection. My feelings for you are completely different, Megan. I *really* love you. We're alike in so many ways. You're like a part of me." He looked deep into her eyes. "I promise I would never knowingly hurt you, and I want us to be together always." He hesitated for a long moment.

"This isn't quite how I intended it. I wanted it to be more romantic. I'd intended to wait until my divorce became final, but it's driving me insane waiting to ask you." He drew a deep breath. "Megan, as soon as my divorce does come through, and I'm free, will you marry me?"

She stared at him, wide-eyed, without answering, and his heart missed a beat. Had he presumed too much? He'd promised her they'd take it slow, and now here he was proposing marriage—after admitting his first marriage had been a disaster.

"Yes, oh Glyn, yes, of course I will. I'll be proud to marry you," she whispered at last. "You know I love you—and I'll love Huw too, as if he were my own son. In fact, I already do, I promise."

"I know you do." He drew her close again and ran his fingers through her hair, hardly believing this sweet, beautiful woman had just agreed to marry him, even if they did have to wait for his divorce to be finalised before they could officially announce their engagement.

"Huw has grown very fond of you, too, you know. He will be so happy when we tell him." He kissed her again, a long, tender kiss which it seemed neither of them wanted to end.

And, as he held her close, he noticed the subtle fragrance of lavender wafting through the open window.

Epilogue

March 1st (St. David's Day)

The bright rays of sunshine on a glorious spring morning illuminated the stained-glass windows of the old Methodist chapel, throwing rainbow shadows on the path. Glyn smiled at his beautiful bride, his heart filled with tenderness and pride.

"A kiss for the wedding album?" the photographer suggested, and Glyn needed no more encouragement.

In her full-length silk gown, Megan looked like a fairy tale princess. The sweetheart neckline of the bodice, trimmed with lace, showed off her curves to perfection. A band of sparkling crystals emphasized her narrow waist, and intricate, embroidered flowers embellished the full, flowing skirt. A long, delicate lace veil, with scalloped edges, and a circlet of creamy white rosebuds covered her hair, which she wore down in waves, past her shoulders.

They ended their kiss, and he gripped her hand tightly, half afraid he was dreaming, and she might suddenly disappear like a mirage.

"Now let's have the bridesmaids and the best man and pageboy as well."

Huw, looking very proud and smart, if a little self-conscious, in a dark suit, white shirt and tie, dashed up to stand next to Glyn and Evan.

The couple had decided on a small, early spring wedding, with just their close friends. They were both sad Megan's mother and father were no longer alive to see her on her wedding day, but Glyn's parents had travelled over from Anglesey. They'd met Megan a couple of times when Glyn took her Anglesey to visit them for a few days, leaving the farm in Evan's capable hands. They made it plain they loved her the moment they met her, and welcomed her into their family, more than happy to see him marry someone his father termed *the right woman.* Glyn made them promise to visit him and Megan at Hafod Farm, whenever they were able to, relieved their previous rift was now well and truly in the past.

****

Megan closed her eyes for a second, wondering what she had done to deserve to be so happy. She glanced down at her bouquet of white rosebuds, carnations and sprigs of lavender, tied with a pale blue satin ribbon finished with a large bow. She was pleased she'd had the idea of adding lavender to her bouquet. The purple sprigs looked very pretty and gave off a delightful scent. Her diamond and sapphire engagement ring sparkled in the sunlight, beside her new, gold wedding ring.

Her bridesmaids, Bethan, Catrin and Mair stood beside her, smiling at the camera. They wore ankle-length lavender-blue gowns, with posies of cream and pale pink rosebuds, blue irises and baby's breath, tied with lavender satin ribbons

Glyn gripped her hand tightly, and she gazed at him, feeling her cheeks glow with happiness. He looked even more handsome in his silver-grey morning suit, white shirt and silvery cravat, with a buttonhole of white rosebuds and lavender to match her bouquet. She hadn't seen him in a suit very often, but he carried it off as if he wore it every day. He slid his arm around her waist, and she looked up at him, scarcely able to believe this wonderful, gentle man really was now her husband.

"And another one of the bride and groom. Big smile please!"

As if it were possible for her to smile any more broadly.

****

"Does she not look beautiful?"

"She does indeed, my little matchmaker. Are you happy now you have accomplished what you set out to do?"

"Of course, I am. I love a happy ending, and those two were truly meant for each other. They just needed a little encouragement."

Rhiannon and Sion drifted hand in hand, mingling unseen with the guests. When all the photographs had been taken, the happy couple rode to the wedding feast in an open carriage, drawn by two perfectly matched cream-coloured Welsh ponies. The rest of the guests followed by more modern means, leaving Rhiannon and Sion to reflect on the events of the past twelve months.

"I am so glad Megan decided to keep the cottage and rent it out to someone else who will enjoy living there, now she'll be living at Hafod Farm."

"Another lonely soul for you to practice your matchmakin' on?"

Rhiannon giggled, a sound like the water in the brook chuckling its way through the little copse behind the chapel.

"Perhaps. You know Sion, there were times when I thought those two would never get together."

"You do not fool me, Rhiannon. You with your schemin'. You were determined to make it work."

"Yes, I was, but 'twas not always easy, especially when Clarissa turned up. I really thought she was going to ruin things for a moment, but thankfully her greed was stronger than her professed mother-love—or even her lust for Glyn."

"Lust?" *Sion turned and gave her an enquiring look.*

"Yes, Sion dear. Anyone could see she never truly loved him, or anyone except herself—and I imagine she never will. She did not really love Glyn, but she did lust after him and could not stand the thought of him being happy with someone else. I expect her to have a string of lovers and to grow into a rich, but lonely old woman, but 'tis her own fault. To be sure Glyn will forgive her, and Huw is such a sweet-natured boy, he will too. In time, he will visit her, but they will never be close, and he will always look to Megan for the love and guidance his mother should have given him."

"And can you predict any more of the future?"

Rhiannon did not answer for a moment. "You know I do sometimes have visions of the future, yet I cannot predict the future with any real certainty. However, if I could, I would predict a future full of love and happiness for Megan and Glyn, and two children, a boy and a girl. Both will inherit their father's love of horses and be a joy to their parents and their half-brother. With Glyn's encouragement and support, Megan will be able to achieve her dream of being an artist. Also, it will take time, but eventually Glyn will have his riding school." She gave a soft laugh. "You know, I feel so sure of all that, perhaps I really can predict some things!"

"And what about us, cariad?"

Rhiannon turned and drifted into his arms. To anyone watching, it might have looked like soft wisps of mist swirling together, but to Rhiannon and Sion, their arms around each other felt as solid as the trunks of the old oak trees they glided past.

"Have faith. You and I, Sion, will keep helping people find love, until we have earned our angel status and can finally enjoy a peaceful afterlife for eternity. Although," she added with a grin, "I will not mind if we must wait a while. After all, what better calling could an angel in waiting have than to be a matchmaker?"

A word about the author...

Horse and dog lover, incurable romantic, and virtual star traveller, Hywela Lyn lives in a small village in England, although her heart remains in her native rural Wales, which inspired much of her writing. Her pen-name, Hywela Lyn is a combination of her first two names. (She has always been known by her second name 'Lyn' and thought it was time her Welsh first name was used as well!)

When not writing or reading, she can usually be found enjoying the outdoors with horses and her 'rescue' dog Choccy - or just eating chocolate!

She is a member of The Romantic Novelists' Association and her local writing group, Chiltern Writers. She loves hearing from readers and fellow authors and can be contacted through her website: Hywelalyn.co.uk

Thank you for purchasing
this publication of The Wild Rose Press, Inc.

For questions or more information
contact us at
info@thewildrosepress.com.

The Wild Rose Press, Inc.
www.thewildrosepress.com

www.ingramcontent.com/pod-product-compliance
Ingram Content Group UK Ltd.
Pitfield, Milton Keynes, MK11 3LW, UK
UKHW031128120325
456135UK00006B/37